Forever Bound

Bondage Erotica

mischief

This novel is entirely a work of fiction.
The names, characters and incidents portrayed in it are
the work of the author's imagination. Any resemblance to
actual persons, living or dead, events or localities is
entirely coincidental.

Mischief
An imprint of HarperCollins*Publishers*
77–85 Fulham Palace Road,
Hammersmith, London W6 8JB

www.mischiefbooks.com

A Paperback Original 2013

First published in Great Britain in ebook format by
HarperCollins*Publishers* 2012

Find out more about HarperCollins and the environment at
www.harpercollins.co.uk/green

CONTENTS

Ring My Bell
Rose de Fer

I don't like the way he's eyeing the ropes.

No, that's a lie. If I'm honest, I do like the way he's eyeing the ropes. A lot. And I can't help the little tingles of pleasure and the weakness in my knees as I imagine what he could do with them. But there's no way I can admit that to him. No, my fantasies are my own dirty little secrets, nothing I could ever share with another person.

But here's the thing. Do I really have to admit it to him? Can't I just feign nonchalance and pretend I'm not desperate to know how it feels to have my wrists bound and stretched up over my head, the position forcing me onto my toes? To have my ankles tied to the bedposts and my legs spread wide so I can't close them? To have my long hair twisted and twined into an elegant knot and secured to a bar that holds my head in place? Can't he just read my mind?

1

If these images sound specific it's because I've down-loaded a few photos. Well, more than a few. Probably hundreds. I live in mortal terror of a computer crash that will send me to the data-recovery experts who will get a privileged glimpse into my private fantasy world. Or perhaps more than a glimpse. What if one of them found the pictures as arousing as I do and perused the whole extensive library? Would I be able to tell from the knowing grin as the guy handed my laptop back to me? What if he happened to be an expert rigger who was looking for someone willing to submit to his coils and knots? What if …

Oh, who am I kidding? That would never happen. That's the sort of 'meet cute' that only happens in cheesy romcoms. And anyway, why am I thinking about some nonexistent computer geek shibari master when Brian is weighing the lengths of spare rope in his hand and looking up at the bells like that? More to the point, why is he looking at *me* like that?

Blushing, I avert my gaze, peering up into the tower as if I'm fascinated by the bells. In actuality what I'm fascinated by are the long ropes descending from them and held teasingly out of reach. They might be the legs of a fluffy multicoloured octopus suspended over our heads.

'Pretty,' I say. It's an empty, meaningless word, just something to fill the silence.

'Have you ever rung bells?' Brian asks. He puts the coil of rope back on the scarred wooden table by the font and moves to my side.

'No,' I say. Then I remember. 'Well, kind of. One time. When I was a kid.' At his expectant look the embarrassing memory returns and I look down at my feet.

Brian laughs. 'You got pulled off your feet, didn't you?'

I cover my face and nod, remembering the humiliation of the event. I'd only thought to ring the bell once and scamper away before anyone saw me. But the bell had other ideas. The vicar told me off, my sisters laughed at me and my parents looked as ashamed as if I'd spat on the altar.

'You're adorable when you're embarrassed,' Brian says, which only embarrasses me further. My face is burning.

'So you know how to ring bells?' I ask, desperate to change the subject.

'I'm sure I haven't forgotten. My uncle and I used to help ring the changes here when I was a boy.'

The image seems incongruous. Somehow I can't picture Brian doing anything so churchy. With his ripped jeans and long hair and Celtic tattoos he seems out of place here. But perhaps he was once a rosy-cheeked choirboy, just as I was once a fresh-faced little girl in plaits.

He runs a hand through his hair and I watch the simple gesture, remembering the feel of his hands on me in the club the night we met. We weren't able to shout over the pounding dance beat but we managed to communicate well enough without our voices. And we'd spent the last few hours before the sun came up in a nearby Travelodge, where we didn't sleep at all. Neither of us was keen to return to our respective mundane jobs in the morning but we kept each other company with rude texts throughout the day, reminiscing over our antics the night before. It kept me sane until the evening, when we could meet up again.

We had dinner, then each other. I was only halfway out of the sleeves of my stretchy red top when he pushed me down on his bed and kissed me hard. In that one moment I felt a wave of excitement beyond anything I'd ever known. I was completely helpless until he drew back to strip me the rest of the way and all night I kept hoping he'd pin me down or suggest some other way of restraining me.

A scene popped into my head from a film I'd seen where a man asked his lover, 'May I blindfold you?'

'Don't ask her,' I'd moaned at the screen in frustration. 'Just do it!'

I imagined Brian asking me politely if he might tie me up and it was like someone had thrown ice water over the fantasy. He knew my body so well already; how could he not know what was in my subby little mind? He shouldn't need to ask; he should just know.

A muffled bong snaps me out of my reverie and I

blink in surprise, forgetting for a moment where I am. All those sleepless nights catching up with us, no doubt. Well, me anyway.

Brian has released one of the long bell ropes and my eyes go wide as he takes hold of the fluffy grip.

'Brian, don't –'

But instead of the noisy clang I'm expecting, the bell only makes another soft bong.

'It's OK,' he says. 'The clappers are muffled.'

'So what's the point of ringing them?'

'Oh, I don't intend to ring the *bells*.'

Something in the way he says it makes it sound wicked. Did he really emphasise the word 'bells'?

'Then what ...' My voice trails off as he fishes a large key out of his pocket and heads for the door.

A thousand thoughts flash through my mind at once. I've only known this guy for a few days and I've hardly slept since meeting him. He could be a psycho for all I know. He was vague about his job when I asked him what he did; maybe he doesn't even have a job. Maybe what he does is seduce girls and suggest he show them this lovely old church, lock them in and slash them to ribbons on the altar in some blood-soaked Satanic ritual.

Maybe. But somehow I don't think so. Even if my judgement is impaired through lack of sleep, my body has its own instincts and it knows what it wants. What I want. And I want whatever he is about to do to me.

I watch silently as he turns the key in the ancient door. The tumblers clank home like the lock of a jail cell and my legs begin to tremble. Then, smiling, he pockets the key and returns to where I stand beneath the raised tentacles of the bell ropes. One by one he lifts them down until the fluffy grips dangle free, encircling me. I feel like an animal caught in a brightly coloured cage.

He smiles at me as he raises my right arm and loops one of the bell ropes around it. With a look he tells me to hold my arm still and I obey the wordless command, watching transfixed as he constructs a cradle with the thick rope, winding it around itself and knotting it above. I could easily slide my arm free of the loose loop but I suspect there is more to come.

He does the same with my left arm and I test the strength of the ropes by gently leaning back and tugging down. The two bells I'm tethered to respond with a muffled ringing and Brian smiles.

'Very nice,' he says.

I press forward for a kiss and he obliges me. Warm wetness pulses between my legs. All my life I've dreamed of an encounter like this. I'm familiar with the sensation of rope against my skin, but only from inept experimentation. On my own. It's just not possible to tie yourself up in any convincing or arousing way without feeling a little silly or worrying what will happen if someone barges in unexpectedly. Or even worse: if you get stuck. I've ruined all such private moments with the 'what if' image of me hobbling to the phone and trying to dial 999 with my nose.

Brian brings me back to the moment with another kiss. Something in his eyes says he knows my frustrations and desires. Perhaps he's felt it too in his own way.

When he pulls away at last he pushes my short skirt up around my waist. I glance nervously around, half expecting to be accosted by an outraged vicar. Is it blasphemous, what we're doing? Even if I were one of the faithful flock I doubt I'd be bothered by this stage. Not when a lifelong fantasy is about to come true.

'Don't worry,' Brian says. 'We're alone. I've locked us in.'

His words chill me as much as they reassure me. I am completely at his mercy and we'll be undisturbed for however long he intends to play with me.

He takes hold of another rope, loops it around my right thigh and pulls it taut. The tail of the rope is coarse and scratchy but the woolly handgrip is too high up for this job. The layered coils he winds around my leg create a wide band of support and I relax and watch him work. At one point he brushes the gusset of my knickers with the rope and I moan softly.

Again he ties an elaborate knot somewhere out of sight above me and then he repeats the process with my left leg. Both ropes are wound several times around my upper thighs, holding me securely, but I'm not quite as trapped as I'd imagined I'd be, since I could still pull my arms free if I wanted to.

He seems to read my puzzlement in my face because he gives me a wicked grin. Then he takes hold of the ends of the ropes he tied my legs with and begins to pull. And I give a startled little cry when I feel my feet lift off the stone floor. I gasp and kick my legs in surprise, losing a shoe in the process.

'Be still,' he says chidingly.

I do as he says. I clutch the soft grips on the arm ropes and the wide loops take the weight on my underarms as the position tips me back. He raises my legs just off the floor until I'm sitting in a sort of sling. The position draws my legs apart and if I try to push them together the bells chime softly above me.

'Comfy?' Brian asks casually.

I'm too astonished to speak. The sensation of being raised up off the floor is both scary and exciting. I make some sort of sound, a mousy little squeak he clearly knows how to read. I suspect he's done this before. But instead of feeling jealous at the thought of past girlfriends, the idea excites me even more. I imagine him tying up a succession of girls, approving of the responses of some, finding fault with others. All at once I feel like a harem girl who dreams of being the sultan's favourite. I am determined not to disappoint him. Like an obedient slave, I want to make him proud.

Brian smiles at me and crosses to the table, where he picks up two coils of thinner rope. 'Like I said, I used to ring the changes here when I was a boy. That meant hours of practice, often on my own. So I found ways to make it more interesting.'

He unwinds them and moves around behind me. I feel him take hold of my foot and I wiggle my toes as he slips off my remaining shoe and places it beside the other. The rope rasps against my ankle and I tremble as I stare around me at the church. I can't help imagining rows of stern-faced parishioners sitting in the pews, turning round to look at me. I might be some innocent peasant girl on trial for witchcraft, at the mercy of the villainous witchfinder who must restrain me to do his duty.

My sex throbs wildly with each fantasy as Brian knots the rope around my ankle and draws it back behind me, securing it to the rope around my thigh. Finally, with both my ankles secured, I realise I can't close my legs at all. My knickers feel shockingly wet in the cool air of the church and I shudder in anticipation as I listen to him walking around behind me.

At last he returns to face me and I wonder if he is pleased. I hang before him as though I'm kneeling in midair, my legs splayed, my crotch at the level of his chest. And all the while, the bells produce their muffled peal above us with every tiny movement I make. I wonder if anyone can hear it outside the church?

9

He stands between my legs and gazes at my silky pink knickers. My arousal is more than obvious. With a finger he traces a line from one bent knee up along my bare thigh and across the loops of rope. I shudder with pleasure as he draws his finger up the soaked little crease. He teases me, stroking me through my sodden knickers, flicking my clit and pressing his knuckle against the warm wet centre of my sex, the place that hungers for penetration.

I long for him to slip his finger underneath the elastic, to tear away the sheer material that separates us. The bells register my frustration as I twist in my bonds, straining with my hips to press harder against his questing fingers.

Then he moves away and I whimper with longing, not daring to beg him or make demands. Some primal instinct tells me I must wait for his favours and rewards. Like a good little slave, I think, and the thought makes me even wetter.

He returns with another rope and this one he fastens to the tangle of knots that bind my legs. It drops it down between my folded knees, where it hangs for a moment, loose and limp. But the look in his eye tells me that this rope is not as innocuous as it looks. And I understand when he swishes the frayed end of the rope through the air like a whip and then flicks it sharply against my pussy.

I yelp, more out of surprise than pain. The little stroke makes my cunt throb and I hold my breath as he raises the rope again. He brings it down briskly on my swollen mound and this time I cry out in earnest. I struggle in my bonds but there's no way I can escape the sweet torture. Again and again he inflicts it on me and each time I feel my sex burn more fiercely in response. My knickers are drenched by the time he finally stops but he isn't finished with me yet.

He draws the rope tight up against my sex and feeds it around behind me, forcing me to straddle it. He tightens it slowly, increasing the pressure until he is satisfied. The rope vibrates slightly as he secures it behind me. The pressure against my clit is immediately almost more than I can take. I whimper, writhing helplessly, but every movement only serves to increase the friction, to stimulate me further.

Gasping and panting, I feel each little throb the rope forces from my tender sex. Brian's hands reach around me from behind to clasp my breasts, and my nipples tighten like pebbles inside my T-shirt. I'm not wearing a bra and his fingers find the hard little knots and close around them, pinching them cruelly.

I throw my head back and arch my back, crying out as the crotch rope presses into me again. I'm lost somewhere between pain and pleasure and I don't know which is which any more.

He drags the front of my shirt up to expose my breasts and then pulls it the rest of the way up over my head, anchoring it behind my neck so my breasts are fully on display. Goose flesh springs up along every inch of bare flesh but it's not from the chilly air of the church. My muscles quiver, straining against the unfamiliar position. Every movement, however small, triggers an equal response from the ropes binding me. It is as though the ropes are a living creature, one that tightens its grip on me with each little struggle.

Brian kneads my breasts from behind, playing with my nipples and kissing the back of my neck. My skin tingles all over and the crotch rope is in danger of wrenching a powerful climax from me already. Apparently sensing my nearness, Brian stops and loosens the rope. I whimper in protest.

'No, no,' he says with a chuckle.

Bereft of its stimulation, my clit throbs even more insistently, its pulses so desperate they almost hurt. There is nothing in the world I want more right now than to come and I wriggle and squirm to beg for it with my body.

'Please,' I whisper.

But he is a cruel, teasing master. 'Not yet,' he says firmly.

The authority in his voice makes me melt and I close my eyes, abandoning myself to whatever further torments he has in mind. I'm desperate for release but at the same time I never want the moment to end.

I moan with frustration until I hear the sharp snick

of a blade. My heart leaps like a fish in my chest but I force myself to keep my eyes closed. He wants me to trust him and I do. Completely.

'Stay perfectly still,' he tells me, his voice a silky whisper in my ear.

I nod to show him that I will, demonstrating with my stillness that I will do whatever he tells me, that I am completely his.

There is the icy bite of cold steel against my bare thigh and I grit my teeth, willing myself to be absolutely still. He draws the blade along my trembling skin before slipping it beneath the edge of my knickers. The wispy silk falls away to one side and I writhe a little at the exposure. He slices through the other side and I am completely exposed for him.

'Good girl,' he says, rewarding me with the touch of his warm fingers against my swollen clit.

I gasp and roll my hips, my thighs quivering and straining with the position. But the helplessness is exquisite.

With both thumbs he spreads the lips of my pussy and my face burns hotly at the exposure. He teases the wet opening of my vagina and I nearly scream when he finally slips a finger inside. He swirls it around inside me and my body feels electrified. I throw my head back with a gasp and look up into the tower. If only the bells were free of their muffles; their wild jangling might serve as the voice of my body, filling the air with an unrestrained peal of ecstasy.

I flash back on all the orgasms he has given me over the past few days and nights. After each I was certain there could never be another one as intense, as knee-tremblingly euphoric. And each new one proved me wrong. If I weren't suspended as I am, I have no doubt that my legs would give way in response to what he's doing to me now.

I feel the pads of his thumbs on either side of my clit, pressing gently against it, circling it, sweeping across it. When he lowers his mouth to me I know it will only be a matter of seconds. The warm wetness of his tongue flicks across my clit as he splays my lips wide with his fingers. Then he closes his lips around me and sucks the hard little bud into his mouth. Sudden bright pain blossoms into pleasure and it takes me a moment to recover from the surge of sensation. He does it again and I feel his fingers slide closer and closer until he fills me again, this time with more than one. He draws his head back and brushes the tender head of my clit with his lips, exhaling hot breath on it before lapping gently at it again. At the same time he draws one wet finger down the dewy crease of my sex and up between my clenching cheeks. And as he tongues my clit with his fingers deep inside me, I feel him slip another finger into my arse.

The combination of sensations overwhelms me and I

surrender to the most powerful orgasm I've ever experienced. Not caring who hears, I send a wild and primal scream up into the tower. The bells may be gagged but I'm not. I thrash in my bonds, securely restrained and powerless, at the mercy of devastating waves of ecstasy.

When the last little throbs finally begin to diminish, I lie panting in my cage of ropes, swaying gently back and forth as my body tingles and tiny fireworks dance behind my eyes. I let go of the fluffy grips and the ropes support me under my arms. Limp and utterly spent, I feel as weightless as an astronaut adrift in space. I could just float here forever.

I don't know how long Brian waits before speaking. Minutes? Hours? Days? I have absolutely no sense of time and I barely even recognise my own name when he says it. But I can feel my limbs beginning to protest, and the tingling eventually brings me back down to earth even though it's the last place I want to be.

I'm struggling to find words but when I see the delighted expression on Brian's face I realise I don't need to say anything at all. All my shame has been purged and I don't care what a lewd exhibition I make, splayed and exposed and suspended from the bell ropes of a little village church.

The pins and needles remind me that there is a price for everything and Brian holds me as he unties me and gently eases me down onto the floor. Once there, I curl into a foetal position, still buzzing from the experience. He replaces all the ropes as though concealing evidence of a crime and I close my eyes as the bells at last fall silent, their muffled peal fading with the last twinges of my climax.

I think of all the pictures on my hard drive. All the elegant, artistic Japanese ones; the rough and functional damsel-in-distress ones; the rude and nasty hardcore ones. I had my favourites, of course. The reliable ones I'd return to again and again for inspiration when I clicked through them with one hand on the mouse and one on my vibrator. Suddenly they all seem bland and boring. Not a single one of them can compare to what I've just experienced.

Rope marks are imprinted on my skin and in some places I can feel bruises.

'Don't worry,' Brian says, misreading my expression. 'They'll fade in a few hours.'

I wrap my arms around his neck and kiss him. 'No,' I say. 'Promise me they never will.'

Roped In
Medea Mor

Emma Grafton was wrapping up the tiramisu her mother had asked her to bring when she heard her husband's voice behind her.

'Strip.'

She turned around, a little disbelieving. Connor stood in front of her, holding a large coil of rope in his hands. The smile playing across his lips told her he had plans for her, the kind that usually involved either tons of patience and discomfort or copious amounts of sweat and semen. Unfortunately, they didn't have time for such plans. They were supposed to be at her parents' in an hour, to celebrate her brother John's thirtieth birthday. The whole extended family had been invited, and her mother had insisted that they come early. She couldn't believe Connor had forgotten about the party, especially after she'd been slaving away in the kitchen to prepare the tiramisu that was a favourite with all her nephews and nieces.

'You're aware that we have to be at my parents' in an hour, right?' she asked, trying to keep her voice neutral. She wasn't questioning his judgement; she was just reminding him of something that appeared to have slipped his mind. He wouldn't take offence at that, would he?

'Very aware,' he assured her. He grinned at her with the nonchalance that had stolen her heart six years earlier. It still affected her today, after five years of marriage, mostly because she'd come to associate it with their weekend sexcapades. This was the grin he reserved for when he was about to do dirty things to her – the sort of things that tended to take more time than they had at present.

'So ... maybe we shouldn't be doing this now,' she suggested.

The grin disappeared, only to be replaced with a frown. 'Are you being contrary, Em? I thought we had rules about that.'

Oh, they had rules, all right. Rules which stated that they were equals during the week, but that she was to obey him in everything on the weekends. Generally, she loved obeying him, to the point where looking forward to the weekend had taken on an entirely different dimension since she'd met him. But this was a special circumstance. It was John's birthday, and she didn't want to be the person who showed up an hour late for the festivities. Not today. Lord knows she'd done it too many times in the past.

However, one look at Connor's increasingly stern face taught her the error of her ways. Whatever he had in mind, he seemed to have set his heart on it and, when Connor had set his heart on something, it was best not to mess with him. Not on a weekend, anyway. Emma had learned that to her detriment on a few occasions. She'd had trouble sitting afterwards.

With a sigh, she took off the top she was wearing, then the elegant grey trousers she saved for special occasions. Her eyes were focused on Connor's as she unfastened her bra and stepped out of her knickers. When she was naked, she assumed the position he'd taught her. Standing tall, she pulled her shoulders backwards, thus making her breasts more prominent. She pressed her heels together and did her best to lengthen her neck. Then she put her hands behind her back, assuming that Connor would want to bind them. He usually did.

He surprised her, though. 'Lift your arms sideways, feet slightly apart,' he ordered.

She obeyed, and watched with bated breath as he uncoiled the rope, a good thirty feet of thickish hemp. Hemp was tricky, she knew. It held knots extremely well, but could be abrasive, even though Connor had done his best to make it less so. She'd sat next to him as he'd burned off loose fibres and had endlessly sanded the rope in order to make it smoother. It was much smoother now than when he'd bought it, but it still irritated her skin when she struggled too much. 'That's the idea,' he had explained to her with a mischievous smile when she'd had the audacity to complain. 'To teach you motionless submission and prevent you from struggling.'

She watched a little nervously as he folded the rope in half and slid the loop around her neck. Two inches below her collarbone he tied the two lengths together in a large, flat knot. He then proceeded to tie three more roughly equidistant knots, until the rope reached her pussy, where he re-tied his most recent knot several times before he appeared to be satisfied with it. Then, smiling at her as if it was the most natural thing in the world, he slid the rope between her labia and, stepping behind her, pulled it backwards through her legs. She could feel it tightening in her crotch and arse crack as he lifted it and began to tie more knots in it behind her back. Then he looped it underneath the rope at the back of her neck, leaving her with a vertical line down both her front and her back.

She knew now what he was making. It was going to be a *karada*, a decorative rope harness in the Japanese style. He'd practised it on her a couple of times before, on both occasions turning her into artfully trussed meat.

From here, she knew, the two ends of the rope would

be separated again, and each end would be wrapped around one side of her waist, weaving back and forth between the central rope on her front and the one on her back until her skin was criss-crossed with lines. There would be diamond shapes and triangles and interesting geometrical patterns. It would be a veritable piece of body art, one which no one but the two of them would ever see, but of which Connor would be rightly proud.

As he walked around her, directing the ropes between and underneath her breasts to create a hemp bra, she watched his fingers, so meticulous and assured. With great dexterity, he slipped an end of the rope into the space between two knots on her belly and pulled it backwards again to loop it into a similar space on her back. He repeated this process several times, moving further down with each repetition. She watched transfixed as the diamond shapes began to take form on her belly, luxuriating in the sensual feel of the rope sliding across her skin.

She'd heard *karadas* described as rope prisons. She herself didn't think of them that way. To her, a *karada* was a caress, a hempy kiss to go with the sweet caresses Connor would occasionally bestow on her neck and breasts as he arranged and re-arranged the ropes. She relished the intimacy of the experience, the perfection of the patterns, the meditative ambience that Connor had assured her was the most important aspect of bondage.

Most of all, however, she relished the way the crotch rope shifted each time he looped an end beneath it. It wasn't long before she found herself responding to the movement, feeling chills of pleasure run up her spine with each subtle shift. And then, suddenly, Connor stopped.

'Aren't you ... aren't you going to bind my arms?' she asked a little hesitantly when the harness was complete and Connor had tied the ends of the rope on her back.

He looked at her, his head cocked to one side. 'Do you really want me to deliver you at your parents' doorstep naked and with your arms tied behind your back?'

She chuckled at the notion, a little embarrassed. 'No, I guess not. But what ...?' Her voice trailed off as she saw his face.

'You're going to go to your parents wearing this *karada* under your clothes, to remind you that you are bound and bonded to me, and that only I can set you free. You're going to feel my hand on you even when I'm not physically touching you. And wait ...'

He walked to the dinner table and came back with a pair of nipple clamps that he had apparently removed from his toolbox while she'd been busy wrapping up her four bowls of tiramisu. To her relief, they were tweezer clamps, which weren't too painful. Of course, their relative painlessness did have a downside, which was that Connor often made her wear them for several hours on end, which *was* uncomfortable.

22

She waited patiently as he played with one of her nipples to make it stiff, then attached a clamp and slid the ring sideways to determine the amount of pressure. He repeated the process with the other nipple. Then he stepped back to admire her from a little distance, looking satisfied with his own work. 'Yes, that will do nicely. Now go and get dressed. The purple skirt, I think. A top that fully covers the harness. No underwear, no stockings. And don't put up your hair. I want it down.'

She nodded respectfully and spoke the words he wanted to hear whenever he gave her a direct order. 'Yes, Connor.' Once in the bedroom, she found the loose purple skirt he had specified, plus a thick black sweater which she thought would do a good job of hiding the harness underneath. As she slipped into the skirt, the crotch rope dug into her arse crack, an unsubtle reminder of its existence. For the time being, though, the nipple clamps were a greater source of discomfort than the harness.

When she was fully dressed, she turned around in front of the mirror to see if the rope and clamps were visible underneath her clothes. After satisfying herself that they weren't, she went back into the living room and presented herself to Connor, who subjected her to an equally thorough examination.

'OK,' he judged eventually. 'Now let's get on the road.'

As she slid into the passenger seat, Emma once again felt the rope dig into her crotch, a feeling that was both

23

uncomfortable and surprisingly pleasant. With a start, she realised that the bottom knot was right on her clit. No doubt that was intentional. Connor wouldn't have redone that knot several times if he hadn't intended it to be exactly where it was.

'How long will I be wearing this?' she asked, trying to hide her excitement by making small talk.

'For the duration of the party and our drive back. Unless you're bad, in which case I'll let you wear it until bedtime.'

Until bedtime. It was a scary thought. Emma didn't think she could wear the harness that long. At some point the hemp would start chafing, and possibly even rupture her skin.

'For my information, what constitutes being bad?'

'Anything that goes against my wishes. Listen to my instructions and you'll be fine.'

So there would be instructions. Bad ones, most likely. The prospect intimidated her a little, but it also sent a thrill of excitement through her.

She remained quiet for the next ten minutes, aware of nothing so much as the knot between her labia. It was right on her clit, and every time she shifted, it pressed down on her like Connor's fingers, except a little drier and itchier. The hemp felt harsh on her tender flesh, but not unpleasantly so.

Feeling experimental, she tilted her pelvis a little, trying to get the knot where she wanted it to be. A thrill shot through her as it hit the right spot. She tried it again, with the same result. Soon she was rotating her pelvis in a series of rhythmic movements, so small that they were barely visible to the human eye. Except to Connor's, obviously.

'Enjoying yourself?' he asked, looking sideways at her. Judging from his smirk, he knew exactly what she was doing. He always did. Undoubtedly he'd been waiting for her to do this, for her to discover the self-pleasuring properties of the rope. No doubt he was hoping to have her randy as fuck by the time they reached her parents'. A little shamefully, she had to admit that it was a distinct possibility.

'It's ... interesting,' she said. She slumped in her seat, which made the rope grow a little tauter between her legs, then brought her pelvis upwards a little. She could barely suppress a moan as the hemp tightened over her clit.

Connor grinned. 'I'm going to have fun watching you this afternoon. Seeing you get yourself off while chatting with your uncles ... I'll gladly suffer your mum's food for the pleasure of that.'

'That's because you're a horrible sadist,' she answered, shifting ever so slightly against the rope.

He just laughed at her. 'Too right, sister. Don't you forget it.'

* * *

As she had expected, Emma was half mad with desire by the time they arrived at her childhood home. She felt a little embarrassed as she congratulated her brother and watched him unwrap the present she'd bought him, a set of Blu-rays of films he'd loved as a child and had said he'd love to watch with his own children. The paranoiac in her was certain that he could smell her arousal or, failing that, would notice she wasn't wearing any underwear, or that there was a chain dangling between her nipples. Who knows, he might even hear some rustling as her thick sweater interacted with the hemp harness underneath. She couldn't hear it herself, but his ears had always been sharper than hers.

However, if John noticed anything out of the ordinary, he didn't let on. Nor did her father, who had an uncanny knack of spotting things that she felt self-conscious about, and a nasty habit of pointing them out in public. Nobody at the party said anything about her looking unusual or uncomfortable; if anything, they seemed to think she was looking healthy and rosy. But, although they didn't seem to notice anything, she was very much aware of Connor's amused glances, and that they made her every bit as wet as the rope and clamps she was wearing.

She soon learned to move as little as possible, so as to prevent the rope from chafing her skin and the chain between her nipples from visibly moving under her clothes. She spent at least half an hour rooted to the same spot, waiting for other people to come to her rather than the other way around. Eventually, though, she had to leave her spot and mingle. It would be rude not to.

As she flitted around the room, chatting now with a cousin, now with an aunt, she was aware of Connor's eyes following her. He smiled every time she shifted her position ever so slightly in an effort to get the knot on her clit in the right spot. He shook his head almost imperceptibly as she scratched herself under a breast, surreptitiously trying to displace the itchy rope that was digging into her skin. He grinned sardonically whenever she glared at him, telling him with her eyes how hard she was finding his torment. And, judging from the bulge in his jeans, he found her predicament as arousing as she did.

Finally, when she found herself without a conversation partner for a moment, he sauntered over to her, turning his back to the other people in the room to hide his erection from view.

'I bet you're sopping fucking wet,' he said under his breath as he handed her a glass of wine.

She coloured, hoping that no one would have heard the words.

'Well? You're dripping, aren't you?'

She nodded, speechlessly.

'Tell me,' he instructed her.

'I ... I'm wet, Connor.' She glanced around, checking whether any of her relatives were within earshot. Only

Aunt Muriel and Uncle Fred seemed to be close enough to be able to hear them, but thankfully, they gave no indication of having overheard anything they shouldn't have.

Her words weren't good enough for Connor, though. He wanted details, as he always did. 'Tell me how wet you are, Emma.'

Flames erupted in her cheeks. She didn't want to be having this conversation in public. It was too embarrassing. And yet she couldn't deny that it was turning her on immensely, as Connor would undoubtedly have known. 'I'm ... I'm very wet, Connor.'

'I suspected as much,' he answered smugly. 'Tell me, my little slut. Are you so wet your juices are running down your thighs?'

Her mouth went as dry as her pussy was wet. She couldn't believe he was doing this to her at a family get-together. She couldn't believe that he had the audacity to be having this conversation in front of so many people, and that she was actually indulging him. 'Yes.'

'Tell me.'

'I ... I'm so wet it's running down my thighs, Connor.' She whispered the last few words in a voice so low that it was barely audible.

'Show me.'

She stared at him, not believing her ears.

'I said: show me. Find yourself a quiet spot, stick your hand between your thighs and show me how wet you are.'

She let out an involuntary groan. 'Connor ...'

'No remonstrations. Go touch yourself, Emma, then show me your hand. Show me what a dirty girl you are.'

Just then, she felt a trickle run down her left thigh, agonisingly slowly but surely. It was ridiculous how wet Connor's games made her.

'Now, Emma.'

She sighed, then took a few sips of wine for extra courage. With her heart pounding in her chest, she put down her glass and made for the toilet, brushing off the two nieces who accosted her. Once inside the small cubicle, she lifted her skirt and put her right hand between her legs. She didn't even have to push the rope aside to feel how extraordinarily wet she was; she could feel the cool moisture pooling on her inner thigh. She ran her hand through it, then pulled her skirt down with her other hand. When she emerged from the toilet, her cheeks were aflame, burning at the thought of what she was about to do.

She walked over to Connor, relieved that he had removed himself from the crowd. He was standing at the table, helping himself to some of the finger food her mother would have spent hours preparing.

She held up her hand for him to see. With a bit of luck, she hoped, it would look from a distance like she was showing him a ring.

He inspected her hand, then her face. 'So fucking wet,'

he murmured appreciatively. 'Go on, lick your fingers, you little tart. Clean those dirty fingers.'

Again, she couldn't help staring at him.

'Lick your fingers for me, Emma,' he repeated in mock exasperation. 'Stick your fingers in your mouth and lick them clean for me, one by one.' She noticed with some alarm that he wasn't even trying to keep his voice down. It was a good thing no one was within five yards of them, or they would have heard his order, loud and clear.

There was nothing for it. She stuck her index finger in her mouth and licked it, slowly and methodically. She experienced the taste of herself on her tongue, a little salty but not disagreeable. It was the taste of her submission, a taste she fully associated with Connor. No other man had ever made her taste herself. No other man had ever got her to do the things he did.

Without taking her eyes off him, she licked her middle finger, then her ring finger, lingering a little longer over her fingertips. She tried not to think of what the other people in the room might be thinking if they happened to be watching her. She tried to ignore the flood between her legs, as well.

'Good girl,' said Connor softly when she had withdrawn the last finger from her mouth. 'I bet you're twice as wet now as before you went to the loo, aren't you?'

You have no idea, she thought. She was so wet that she could feel a steady trickle down her left thigh. If this went on much longer, her wetness would start showing under her skirt. Either that or people would start smelling her arousal from across the room.

'Do you want me to fuck you?' Connor whispered. 'Do you want me to shove my hard cock between your dripping thighs?'

Her heart stopped a moment. With a flash, she realised that this was what he'd intended all along – to fuck her at the parents', after getting her all worked up without anyone even being aware of it. She also realised she'd never needed to be fucked more badly. She needed his cock, pounding her into submission. She needed it *now*.

'Yes, please, Connor,' she whispered. She couldn't bring herself to meet his eyes.

He lifted her chin with a fingertip, forcing her to look up at him. 'Beg me for it,' he commanded. 'Beg me to fuck you, you dirty little slut.'

Her mind went blank. She was reduced to nothing but the throb between her legs, an ache that urgently needed a release.

'Please fuck me,' she whispered. 'Please give me your cock, Connor. I need it.'

He grinned. 'Go upstairs, to your old room. Bend over your desk and lift your skirt. Part your legs. Wait for me.'

She did as he told her. As she climbed the stairs, the rope between her legs dug into her cunt, making her clit pulse like a sore tooth. It was an uncomfortable feeling, but she'd never been randier in her life.

Her childhood room hadn't changed much since the last time she'd seen it. The only difference she noticed at first glance was a pair of suitcases in the corner next to her bed and the stacks of books her parents had placed on her desk. They seemed to have decided to turn her room into a storage space for things that didn't fit elsewhere in the house.

She placed half of the books on the floor beside the desk, and pushed the others to the side. Then she bent over the desk, wincing as the rope grew even tauter between her thighs. There'd be some abrasions there the next day, she suspected. Her nipples, too, began to throb even more furiously, as they always did when she bent forwards while clamped. No doubt that was part of the reason why Connor liked having her bend over for him. Knowing him, he'd probably yank the chain between her nipples while fucking her, making her whole body explode with pain and desire.

Propped up on her left elbow, she extended her right arm behind her to lift her skirt and pull it over her back. Then she waited, clenching her thighs rhythmically to hold on to the immense throb inside her.

Connor kept her waiting for a long time. Throughout the wait she wondered if he'd been drawn into a conversation by one of her relatives or if he was just testing her patience. She was painfully aware that he was very much the kind of sadist who'd keep her waiting just because he could.

When she eventually heard footsteps ascending the stairs, she had an irrational fear that it would be her mother, or the nieces who had tried to ambush her earlier. What would they say if they found her like this, greeting them with the sight of her sopping, rope-bisected pussy? She couldn't begin to imagine the embarrassment, the mortification. No doubt her mother would press her to seek a divorce from Connor at once.

Thankfully, the footsteps turned out to belong to Connor. He whistled softly as he entered the room, then closed the door behind him.

'Wow, look at you, Emma. What a gorgeous sight.'

She knew what would happen next. He'd position himself behind her and make endless comments on her appearance, her wetness, her shame. He'd prod her and inspect her, taking his time to do so, while she was burning up, waiting for him finally to give her what she so desperately needed. That was their ritual. The prospect of it frustrated her, but she couldn't deny it turned her on beyond reason.

True to form, Connor slid his fingers along the rope that was splitting her pussy, inspecting the results of his elegant torture device. 'Fuck, you're wet. You can't wait to have my cock in there, can you, dirty girl?' He softly pulled on the rope, making it dig into her flesh even deeper. 'The rope is soaked. I'll have to wash it tonight. I may have to punish you for that, Em.'

So unfair. And yet such an utterly delectable prospect.

'Or alternatively, I may make you wash the rope yourself, to give you a proper appreciation for how insanely wet you get when I tie you up. Would you like that, kitten?'

She couldn't restrain herself any more. 'Please, Connor ...'

'Please what, kitten? "Please let me wash the rope I've soiled with my filthy pussy juice"?' His hand glided upwards, to her bottom, away from the spot where she wanted it to be.

'You know what I mean,' she muttered, a little exasperated. She'd had enough of the foreplay and the shaming. She needed him to fuck and finger her senseless.

'I have no idea. You'll have to be *much* more explicit, kitten.' He patted her backside as if it was a small child in need of some encouragement.

She nearly groaned in frustration. 'Please fuck me, Connor,' she begged. 'Please fuck me into oblivion.'

He chuckled. 'That desperate, eh? All right, you filthy hussy. I'll give you what you want. But first we'll get rid of these nasty clamps, shall we?'

He pulled down her skirt, and his hands crept under her sweater, hot and searching. With a dexterity born of experience, they loosened the clamps before taking them off altogether. The pressure on her nipples disappeared, but as the blood flowed back into them they tingled with

34

lingering sensation, a throb that was even more painful than when the clamps had been on. She squirmed against the table, shocked by the pain, but also by how much her body seemed to crave it.

She was still squirming when Connor pulled down her sweater and lifted her skirt over her back again. The next moment she heard the sounds she'd been waiting for. His belt being undone. His jeans and underwear being pulled down in one swift movement. He put a hand on her hip, then hooked a finger of his other hand under the taut crotch rope and pulled it aside, exposing her slick entrance. She felt the rope dig into the tender skin where her groin met her thigh, but ignored the sensation. The rope was not what mattered now. Her newly exposed entrance was.

He didn't even bother to open her up with his fingers. He just put his cockhead against her opening and pushed it in. She was so wet that he nearly slid out before he was properly inserted, but a second hard thrust solved the problem. No sooner was he inside her than she forgot all about the abrasive rope and the dull ache in her nipples. All that mattered was the cock that was claiming her, giving her what she needed.

He drove into her aggressively, his hands gripping her hips tightly. His hard loins whacked against her buttocks, making an obscene sound that she was sure could be heard outside the room. If anyone were to come upstairs now, they'd have no doubt as to what was happening in her old room.

As Connor rammed himself to her depths, pushing her a little further into bliss with each stroke, she found herself moaning despite her fear of being heard. She couldn't help it; he always had that effect on her.

This time, though, he didn't seem to want to be heard. 'Quiet,' he groaned as he ground his pelvis against her arse.

His next thrust was so hard she actually let out a small shriek, provoking Connor to give her another warning. 'Be quiet, or I'll let you wear this for the rest of the day, until we go to bed,' he hissed. 'I warned you about that, didn't I?'

She didn't answer. Instead, she rode back against him, shifting her buttocks towards him in anticipation of his delicious thrusts.

'I asked you a question, Em. Did I or did I not warn you about wearing this all day if you disobeyed me?' He punctuated the word 'disobeyed' with a ferocious thrust that had her thighs banging against the desk. She could feel the wood digging into her flesh, another indentation to add to the ones created by the rope.

'Yes, Connor,' she managed. 'You did warn me. I'll try to be … quieter.'

'Good. Now finger yourself, slut. Go on, show me how hard you need to come.'

Her fingers flew to her clit, eager to finish the job started by the rope. As he gripped her hips and shoved into her again, she worked her cunt feverishly, in time with his raw thrusts. Gradually, her orgasm built, coming closer with each stroke of his thick cock, each single flick of her fingers. Just then, he twisted his fingers into her hair, pulling her head backwards to him. The pressure on her scalp was enough to bring her to the edge.

'Oh, God,' she moaned. 'God, Connor ...'

He pulled harder, as if to punish her. 'That's it, you noisy slut. You'll be wearing this for the rest of the day. Don't say I didn't warn you.'

She didn't care. All she wanted was to come, right there and then. 'Please ... Please, Connor ...'

'Come,' he commanded. 'Come all over my cock.' He shoved into her again, and the next moment her release exploded through her, all the more intense for having been so long in the making. The muscles in her cunt tightened around him, squeezing his erection. Her whole body went weak, and she was wrenched by the contractions of one of the most powerful orgasms she'd ever experienced. She just managed to swallow the shriek which had been building inside her throat, fearful of what might happen if she let it out.

No sooner had she come than Connor eased his cock from her body. 'On your knees,' he commanded, his voice hoarse with urgency.

She dropped to her knees, ignoring the rope that dug violently into her groin as she did so, and opened her mouth for him. As he jerked himself off in front of her, she couldn't wait to see him explode onto her tongue. She wanted to see the tremor in his thighs just before his semen spurted out of him, just before ...

He shot his load into her. She could feel it pool on her tongue and lips, all soft and runny, and only just managed to resist the urge to swallow it before he was fully done. Eventually, though, she did swallow, feeling the semen go down her throat like a spoonful of salty jelly. His hands tightened in her hair as she sucked his cock dry of its final oozings, cleaning him as she'd like to be cleaned herself. Not for the first time, she realised that she loved his hand in her hair, loved the possessiveness of his claiming her like that. Even more than this ropes, her hair was her leash, the one with which he enforced her absolute obedience.

When she'd got to her feet, he placed the rope between her labia again and helped make her look presentable, pulling down her skirt and smoothing her hair as best he could. 'That was sensational,' he whispered as he put his lips to her forehead. 'I look forward to seeing what the evening will bring.'

The evening. With a pang, Emma realised she'd be wearing the harness for the remainder of the day. Six more hours until bedtime. Six more hours of this itchy, uncomfortable torment, which was leaving marks on her body that would take hours to fade. Oddly, the thought didn't bother her. As they descended the stairs, ready to mingle with her relatives again, she felt the excitement of anticipation settle over her like a fever. The evening wasn't over yet. It was only just beginning, and it was going to be fun. She knew it in the itchy spots beneath the rope, where wisdom lay.

Madeline and More
Giselle Renarde

Madeline chain-smoked two packs a day. Used to be three, but she cut down because she didn't want her skin to start looking like a catcher's mitt.

She reminded me of a white witch. Her hair was long and straggly, and she always had on wispy skirts that brushed her ankles. She usually wore white or grey, or shades of blue and green. Never black, except on stage, which struck me as strange because she was famous for writing requiems.

To look at her, you'd never guess Madeline was a world-famous composer. But I guess people have outdated ideas of what composers look like. The first year our choir collaborated with Madeline, I remember the other sopranos asking, 'How does such beautiful music come out of such a hag?' That hurt me, right to my core, because I thought Madeline was gorgeous.

For four years she'd been writing original choral music for us to premiere at our annual Christmas concert. Having the words 'World Premiere' on the programme certainly helped to put bums in the seats, but I knew she only helped us along because she was sleeping with our choirmaster Diana. Their relationship was brutally obvious.

But something was different this year. When Madeline arrived to hear how we were faring with the new piece, she seemed even more aloof than usual. She swept down the centre aisle of the creepy old church where we rehearsed and threw her purse and her bags on the front pew. She didn't give Diana the usual big hug and kiss. In fact, she didn't so much as glance in our choirmaster's direction.

Something was very, very different. Had they broken up? Oh, the thought made my belly flip. Right away, my mind shot to the possibility of being Madeline's next conquest.

My hands were shaking as I took Madeline's original setting of 'Balulalow' from my music folder. The piece hadn't yet been published, and the vocal score was handwritten. So were the words:

Oh my dere hert, young Jesu sweit,
Prepare thy creddil in thy spreit,
And I sall rock thee to my hert,
To my hert ...
And never mair from thee depart.

Oh, Madeline's handwriting! Madeline's fingers had penned this music, written out those words. Everything that came from her was special and exciting, even a song that had been set famously by Britten and God knows how many other composers.

She sat like a bag lady in the front pew as we sang her work back to her. It was magic. I felt that way about most Christmas songs, but Madeline's new creations brought me to a higher plane of existence. I'd never been a super-religious person, but I'd always loved the focus on music that came about this time of year. The old songs were my favourites, and Madeline's always sounded old even though they were new.

My heart raced as we closed off that final melancholy chord. This wasn't a happy song. Moving, yes, but not celebratory. There was a sense of devotion, of submission. We singers gave ourselves over to the piece as it became a part of us. It was truly an experience of giving in, handing ourselves to Madeline and letting ourselves belong to her.

But what did she think of our performance?

For a moment, she said nothing, did nothing. And then she brought her hands together. She stood and bowed to us, saying, 'Thank you all.'

Her voice was deep and husky from all the years of smoking. She was a choral composer who couldn't sing her own music.

She gave us a few corrections. Some of our pronunciations were too modern but that wouldn't be difficult to change. The main difference was that she wanted to make 'And never mair from thee depart' into a solo soprano line, underscored by the basses and tenors.

'Eva can do it,' Diana offered, and my spine stiffened when I heard my name.

'OK,' I said, feeling the other sopranos sneer. 'I'd love to.'

We all changed our scores. I sang for Madeline and when my voice rang out over the rest of the choir, she smiled. I'd done it. She'd noticed me. We made a connection in that moment, eye to eye, mouth to ear. That moment changed everything.

I stuck around after rehearsal, trying to work up the courage to congratulate Madeline on such a glorious piece. The thought of actually talking to her made me so nervous I had to run to the bathroom. When I returned, my fellow choristers were gone, but I heard two raised voices coming from the room where the church stored choir robes and old furniture, stuff like that. I knew those voices.

Madeline was shouting, 'Take it! I don't want it any more!'

'I bought all that for us,' Diana cried. 'If there is no us, I don't want it either.'

I couldn't help wondering what they were fighting over. My curiosity got the best of me, I suppose, because

43

I came so close to the door I wound up pressing it open with my chest.

Madeline and Diana both looked up when the door squeaked. There was nowhere to hide. They'd seen me.

Diana shook her head and stormed past me, yelling, 'Keep it all or burn it. What do I care?'

I hoped Madeline wasn't mad at me for breaking up their spat. Some people really got off on arguing. But she didn't seem upset. She stared right through me, standing perfectly still except for her thumb, which rolled a silver ring in circles around her middle finger.

'I'm sorry,' I said. 'I just wanted to tell you how much I love your music.'

She looked up and jolted a bit, like she was surprised to see me there. 'Oh. Thank you.'

'It's an honour to be given a solo.'

'Good.' Madeline looked frazzled and frail, and I wished I could do something about that. When she looked at me, I felt like she was staring at a painting, not a person. Finally, she shook her head and her hair exploded around her face. 'I'm sorry. Where are my manners? It's very nice to meet you.'

She extended her hand and I whispered, 'Eva.' There was more silver than flesh on her fingers, but her palm was smooth and cool. Mine was clammy, but she didn't react. 'I always look forward to our Christmas concert because I know I'll get to see you again.'

At first, she didn't react except to nod slowly. Even when she said thank you, I wasn't sure if she'd heard me.

'The Christmas songs you write for us are magnificent,' I said, still hoping to get some reaction. Most women would have given up by now, but Madeline was worth the persistence.

I thought she might say thank you again, but instead she dropped one hand into a bag and pulled out a length of thick black rope. 'Have you ever been tied up?'

That question threw me for a loop, but I answered truthfully. 'Well ... yes.'

'In a church?' she asked.

'Oh. Well ... no.'

'Come here,' she said, wriggling one silver-ringed finger at me. 'Take off your clothes and get up on this desk.'

I'd thought maybe I hadn't communicated how much of a crush I had on her, but she obviously knew. She knew I'd do anything to make her happy, especially when she wore her melancholy like a veil. I stepped out of my frumpy corduroy pants.

'Festive,' Madeline said as I tore off my holly-patterned turtleneck. I felt a little silly, wearing cheery Christmas clothes while Madeline was draped in grey. I felt a lot less silly once I was naked. There's something very serious about nudity, especially when you're in a church.

'Use "yellow light" for slow down, "red light" to stop,' she instructed as I climbed up on the big wooden desk.

'You know it's not smart to give yourself to strangers, don't you?'

'You don't feel like a stranger,' I told her. 'Your music's already inside me.'

She didn't smile, not with her mouth, but a flash of light blazed across her eyes. She told me what to do: sit with both feet up on the desk. Bring my heels in nice and close to my butt cheeks. Place my wrists next to my ankles.

I did everything she asked without question, and I waited patiently as she sorted through the lengths of silky black rope. When they met my skin, I shuddered internally. It felt so good, not only the sensation of rope on flesh, but the knowledge that Madeline was looking at my naked body and thinking about where to tie, where to create those bonds.

She started by securing my wrists to my ankles, then wrapping that lovely rope around my calf, around my thigh, keeping my knees bent. But how to keep my legs apart? I'm sure that's what she was thinking, because the next thing she did was tie another rope around my lower thigh and weave it behind my shoulder, then down my other arm to secure it just above the knee. Now my legs were open for her, and the more I leaned back, the wider they spread.

'Can you move?' she asked.

'No.' I really couldn't. I could wriggle my fingers and my toes, but that was it. 'Thank you.'

'Ahh,' Madeline cooed, finally breaking a slight smile. 'The pleasure is mine.'

I wished I could see myself from her perspective: bound on a desk, legs spread wide, naked pussy drooling and exposed. Did I look too hairy? It had certainly been a while since I'd trimmed down there. And what about my breasts? The right nipple always got much harder than the left one. Would Madeline care that I was so … imperfect?

'I'm glad you enjoy my music,' Madeline said.

'I'm glad you create it.' Stupid thing to say, but it was hard to think on my feet when they were tied to my wrists. 'Can I sing it for you?'

She laughed and pulled a strip of black fabric from one of her break-up bags. 'Why not?'

I sang her setting of 'Balulalow' while she blindfolded me. It didn't have the same effect without the whole choir, but the soprano line carried the melody. Strangely, I felt more naked singing for Madeline than I felt *being* naked, or being tied up with ropes for that matter. Music was such a brutal art. Vocal music, especially. Even when it was desperately beautiful, it still tore through your body like lightning.

'Do you trust me?' she asked when I'd finished her song.

'Yes.' No hesitation.

'God only knows why,' she said. 'But you truly do trust me?'

'Yes.'

'Then drink this.'

She held a bottle to my lip, but didn't tilt it right away. She gave me a chance to ask what it was, but I didn't. In this game, if you trusted your partner you didn't question their actions or requests. You did as you were told.

I drank, and my throat flooded with fresh water. It soothed more than just my vocal cords. That simple action told me Madeline took her duty of care seriously. She would not hurt me, though I couldn't move or see. I already trusted her. Now I knew that trust was not misplaced.

'It's important for a singer to keep hydrated,' she told me. 'And never, never smoke. Do you smoke?'

'No,' I said.

'That's good. It probably costs me a thousand dollars in cigarettes to write one opus. And it'll kill me one day. Never start, because once you start you can't stop.'

'Just like this,' I said, hoping she'd know I meant the power exchange, domination and submission.

Of course she understood. She chuckled deeply and said, 'This I wouldn't give up for the world.'

'Me neither.'

The scent of smoked cigarettes on her skin struck me more deeply now that I couldn't see. Blindfolds always augmented my sense of smell, not to mention my sense of anticipation. I could hear her rifling around in those bags, but I couldn't see what she had in hand. Even as she pulled a chair in close and sat between my legs, I couldn't guess what she was about to do.

Would she lick me? Would she shove something in my pussy? What was she planning?

'Your nipples,' she asked. 'Are they sensitive?'

I gulped. 'Yes.'

'One is harder than the other.'

Of course she had to notice that. 'I know.'

'Do they enjoy being clamped?'

'I don't know if they do,' I said. 'But I certainly enjoy it.'

I laughed, but she didn't.

The clamps met my nipples at exactly the same time, squeezing my poor tits with dull metal teeth. Every sensation was sharper, crisper than when I could see. My temporary blindness brought out beauty in pain.

'How's that?' she asked. 'Not too much?'

'Not too much.' Not yet, anyway.

'How sensitive is your clit?' she asked.

Oh, God! I could already feel the pain from my nipples streaking down between my legs, glowing at the apex of my pussy.

'It's always more sensitive when I've got clamps on my nipples,' I said.

She chuckled, and it sounded like a deep feline purr. 'Good.'

I heard the mechanical whirr of a vibrator and seconds later it was teasing my pussy lips. Oh, she was good.

She knew not to start with my clit. It would have been too much of a shock. Instead she worked her way all around my pussy, stopping just short of my throbbing bud every time.

The vibrator felt super-smooth, and it picked up pussy juice as it circled me, spreading that slick stuff all around. I couldn't believe how wet I'd become, but bondage always did that for me. The second I felt a smooth, thick rope against my flesh, I was ready. My breasts tingled and my pussy throbbed.

'You should see how red your clit looks right now.' Madeline pressed the head of her fake cock just inside my hole, just enough that I could feel its vibrations riding up toward my apex. If I hadn't been tied in knots, I would have thrashed about, maybe even knocked myself off the desk.

There were so many reasons to love being bound. One of the best, aside from giving over personal power to another human being, was the sensation in my muscles when I fought my ties and lost.

'Is your pussy tight?' Madeline asked. She could obviously feel my resistance.

'Yes.' I hugged the vibe with my pussy muscles to show her just how tight I was.

'And how does your pussy taste?' she asked as she forced the fake cock deep inside my cunt. 'Is your pussy sweet?'

Was Madeline going to try it? Oh, I'd give anything to be licked by that woman!

'It's sweet,' I said. 'Sweet like honey. Want a taste?'

Something smacked my breast – an open hand? – and my nipple clamps dug into my flesh. My body sizzled, inside and out. I shrieked. I couldn't help it.

'I'm sorry,' I told her. 'I shouldn't have offered. I shouldn't have assumed.'

She chuckled, and it put me at ease that Madeline hadn't spanked my tits in anger. It was simply a punishment, and one I rightly deserved.

'I'm not going to taste your pussy,' she said.

I couldn't mask my disappointment, and I earned myself another tit-slap that way. The clamps bit down on my nipples, and that pain throbbed in my clit. It hurt so much I screamed, but not so much that I gave her the red light.

Suddenly my pussy was empty and the vibrator was forcing its way between my lips. I'd never had a vibe in my mouth before. I'd sucked a strap-on dildo once, down on my knees, giving it the best blowjob I could manage, but this was different. The strong vibrations made my teeth rattle, but I sucked until my lips went numb.

'Tell me how your pussy tastes,' Madeline cooed. Her deep, sensual voice was one of her most attractive features. It tied my belly in knots.

'Tastes good,' I said around the thick vibe.

She shoved the cock in a little deeper, coating my throat with the heavy musk of my pussy. I tried not to gag. I wanted her to know I could take just about anything.

That's when I heard the squeal of the door. On a gust of wind, I could smell Diana's lilac perfume and without thinking I blurted her name. Of course, my voice was muffled by the vibrating cock lodged in my throat, but I could feel Madeline's tension as she turned.

Even blindfolded, I could see everything that passed between them. I felt every little moment, every drop of pain and desperation. Poor Diana! I felt just awful that she'd walked in on this scene. Even if their relationship was well and truly over, they obviously still loved each other.

'I'm sorry!' I cried around the buzzing cock, but the door closed and there was only quiet. When Madeline took the clamps off my nipples and the vibrator out of my mouth, I said it again. 'I'm sorry.'

'There's no need,' Diana said, and I would have jumped if I hadn't been bound at every angle. She'd closed the door, but stayed in the room. Of course – I could smell her perfume, even sweeter now.

Madeline told her to sit, and I felt Diana's energy move lower. Her knees cracked as she bent all the way down. 'Stay silent,' Madeline said. 'Be good and I'll give you a treat.'

It was strange, imagining my strict choirmaster under

anyone's thumb, but there she was on the floor, playing puppy to Madeline. I hadn't felt weird about Madeline seeing me naked, but my tummy tossed when I pictured Diana staring up at my body bound in black ropes. Was she looking between my legs, or gawking at my tits? Or was she gazing adoringly at Madeline? That's what I'd have been doing, if it were me.

'Have you ever used a pussy pump, Eva?'

A pussy pump? 'No, never.'

'Diana,' she said. 'Find it.'

While my choirmaster hunted through the bags, Madeline filled my throat with more soothing water. I loved this part of submission. I loved being able to count on someone to take care of my basic needs, physical and emotional.

Diana pulled something from a bag and Madeline gasped. 'Ooh, yes, put that on, Diana. Did you find the pump?'

'Right here.'

Madeline made a sound like 'mmmm' and I got so excited my muscles all started to twitch. She laughed, throaty and dark, as she cupped the pussy pump over my mound.

'This usually works better on a shaved pussy, but we'll try it out just to see.'

Diana chuckled in the background, and I felt so ashamed of my hair I wanted to run and hide. No luck.

53

I was stuck there on that desk. I'd given myself over to Madeline and she could do whatever she wanted with me now.

'What does it look like?' I asked, because I knew so little about pussy pumps.

'The cup looks quite like an anaesthetist's mask, except the plastic is entirely clear and it covers your cunt, not your mouth.' Madeline's frigid lust filled me as she spoke. 'Diana will hold it in place while I pump, and that will draw your flesh into the cup like a vacuum.'

I heard the pump wheeze in Madeline's hand a few times before I felt any suction. My knees were beginning to ache from being locked in this awkward position, but I wouldn't complain. I focused on the pressure my favourite composer was generating between my open legs. It seemed more like a dream than real life.

Either my choirmaster was pressing the cup harder against my mound, or the suction from the pump was taking hold. Ooh, yes, I could feel it now. Every time Madeline squeezed the pump and it made that stifled wheezing sound, my pussy felt more pressurised. It was sort of like getting my clit sucked, except the pump acted on more than just my clit. The cup encompassed my entire mound, all the way around my fleshy pussy lips. I imagined this was how it felt to get sucked by an Amazon, one so huge she could stretch her lips all the way over my cunt.

'Her pussy's getting so red!' Diana cried, even though Madeline had told her to stay silent.

Madeline didn't chastise her for speaking, but merely asked, 'Can you feel it, Eva? Does it feel good?'

'Yes,' I panted. The slow sucking was catching up with me, and I could feel an orgasm swirling at the base of my belly. The pump wasn't familiar, but it was certainly effective.

'Tell Eva how her pussy looks now,' Madeline told Diana.

The suction grew so strong my pussy lips felt huge inside the pump cup.

'It's swollen,' Diana said. 'Her pussy is almost purple. Her clit's like a cherry.'

Those words made me writhe against my bindings, but there was no escape. I wanted to fuck something, grind on something. The pump made me hot and horny and super-sensitive, but it wouldn't let me come. God, I wanted to come!

'Take off her blindfold, Diana.'

When Diana removed the satin slip from my eyes, I gasped at what she was wearing: no frumpy choir conductor outfit, not any more. She'd changed into leather pants and a black bustier that scarcely concealed her striking breasts. Diana always wore vests to choir rehearsals. I'd never really thought of her as having breasts at all.

Madeline was still pumping me, and every squeeze was now intolerably tight. My pussy lips felt huge enough to break the plastic cup, and when she removed it Diana held a mirror between my legs so I could see.

'That's me?' I asked, as if it could be anyone else.

'That's you,' Madeline answered.

My pussy lips looked enormous, and they really were swollen and reddish-purple, just like Diana had said. They didn't look real. In fact, the sight of my pussy like that, all distended and huge, made me feel a little squeamish. Madeline must have seen it in my face, because she asked if I'd like my blindfold back on.

'Yes,' I said without hesitation. I could handle the sensation, just maybe not the sight.

Diana tied the blindfold over my eyes, looser than Madeline had, but it still did the job. Once I was back in my world of darkness, I felt much more comfortable. I was all sensation, all lust and desire, and Madeline knew just how to satisfy it.

'Lick her,' she instructed Diana. 'Gently, gently. She's going to be very sensitive.'

My heart raced when I felt my choirmaster's breath on my hot, swollen cunt. I'd wanted Madeline to lick me, but I was so overwhelmingly horny I'd have let anyone get me off.

The moment Diana's tongue met my pussy lips, I arched back with a violence that surprised me. Every time Diana licked my huge clit, I jerked back even harder, and every time I jerked back my thighs spread farther apart. It was hard to imagine my choirmaster's face between my legs. I'd fantasised about Madeline licking my clit, but there was something even more twisted and exciting about Diana doing it at her command.

I fought my ties, screaming as my leather-clad choirmaster lapped my pussy. Her wet tongue sizzled against my skin. The pump had made my lips monstrous and so sensitive that I wanted to buck and writhe, but Madeline's ties held fast. I couldn't move and I couldn't see, and that made me so claustrophobic I started struggling even harder.

Diana's tongue lashed my fat clit hard enough to transform me from a demure chorister to a wild beast. I gripped my ankles, pressing the ropes into my flesh, feeling them bite into my skin. My heart pounded in my ears. The explosions between my legs travelled through my core, and when Madeline placed those metal clamps back on my tits the fireworks were everywhere. Sheer pleasure-pain burst from my nipples to my clit, where Diana worked hard for my exultation.

'Enough,' Madeline instructed, drawing Diana away from my tender pumped-up pussy. I was panting and ecstatic when I felt Madeline's water bottle against my lips. 'Here, baby. Drink up. Drink some water.'

Her deep voice soothed me just like the tepid water

soothed my throat. She was taking care of me, petting my hair, speaking kind words, giving me drink. The care was as good as the pain, but only in conjunction with the pain. For me, one without the other seemed sadly incomplete.

Once Diana had removed my blindfold, both women untied my bonds. My knees ached, locked into the position they'd held far too long. Madeline rubbed her hands together and pressed her hands to my knees, relieving the ache. Her silver rings were hot on my skin, and I almost wished they were hot enough to burn me. I would love to be branded by her.

They let me lie on the desk, creating a makeshift pillow out of my clothes. They kissed my blazing skin with their fingertips. For a while, I listened to them talking about music, performances, nothing in particular. Their voices were the white noise of a relationship in recovery.

I didn't know then that I would fit into their joint existence. I'd placed Madeline on a pedestal and barely noticed Diana, but together as a couple they gave me everything I needed ... and so much more.

The Billiard Room
Tabitha Rayne

'Thank you, don't mind if I do.' Zoe Lake slipped into the finely upholstered chair, making sure to keep her knees locked primly together.

'Milk or lemon?' Lady Tate-Fitzpatrick asked. In one hand she held a small jug, in the other a perfect slice of fruit, hovering over the teacup.

'Oh.' Zoe glanced at the other two women's cups, hoping to get a hint about what would be best in this situation. She plumped for what she'd prefer. 'Milk, please,' she said, smiling as demurely as she could. *I am a businesswoman, I have every right to be here, these people are my clients, they contacted me.* She'd recited her mantra so many times since she got the call to measure up Lady Fitzpatrick's windows for new curtains that she knew it now by its rhythm rather than the words. She'd gone around all four public rooms, each with two huge bay windows, and dutifully and very carefully measured the lot. Her notes were stowed away carefully in her leather briefcase on the Persian rug by her side. Lady Tate-Fitzpatrick's friend had come along to oversee and advise. 'I have appalling taste,' Lady TP had stated by way of explaining the other woman's presence.

Four or five home-interior magazines lay fanned out on the coffee table before them. The Lady reached out with perfect poise and picked one up. 'Well, I suppose we should really think about colour schemes and fabrics. Did you bring your sample book?' she said in the brusque tone that Zoe was only just getting used to. Every time the Lady addressed her, it felt as if she was administering a sharp slap on the hand, and Zoe had to remind herself, every time, that this was just her way.

'Yes, of course, it's in my car, I won't be a sec,' she said, flustered that she'd forgot to bring it in. She rose from her seat and, as she was making her way across the rug, the door opened and a striking silver-haired man popped his head around and addressed the women.

'Are you done yet? I can't be doing with every Tom, Dick and Harry's car cluttering up my driveway ...'

Zoe's breath caught at the back of her throat. She couldn't believe how rude the man had been, and in any other circumstance she would have told him exactly what she thought of his behaviour, but something about the situation made her nervy as a schoolgirl.

'Oh, I … I'm sorry, sir,' she stammered as she came close to him, 'I shan't be long.' His eyes dragged their way from her shoes to her legs, thighs and stomach and lingered lightly at her chest before settling at her lips, which she self-consciously licked. It could only have been a footstep but she felt like the exchange had taken forever. What would his wife say, having her husband eye up another woman so lasciviously? What was he thinking? Zoe ducked under his arm as he held the door open for her, never taking his gaze from her. Crunching her fists and shutting her eyes for a moment, she composed herself, then walked off down the hallway, knowing full well that he was watching her backside and legs. The skin at her throat and décolleté flushed and prickled at being under such scrutiny. But there was something else.

She managed to get to the large heavy door and pulled it open just enough to pass through, then shut it behind her with a clunk. The flush had simultaneously spread up to her cheeks and down to her breasts. Zoe fought the urge to peek at her chest but lost. As she looked down at her breasts in the good blouse, she knew she was in trouble. Her nipples puckered and strained through the fabric, leaving anyone in the vicinity no doubt as to her arousal. What was it about that dreadful man that had her so worked up? She thought of the way he had spoken of his wife's guests with disdain, and the feeling of excitement grew, finding its way down into that deep, welling centre.

Zoe gave her head a brisk shake, freed her hair from its fastenings and raked her fingers across her scalp in an effort to rid herself of these uninvited feelings. *Come on, come on, pull yourself together, you need this contract, come on.* And so her new mantra took shape. One last stamp of her heels and smoothing down of her skirt and she strode off over the gravel to her car, retying her hair on the way. She was very happy with her little MG she'd bought at an auction for a song, and thought that it wasn't too out of place in these grand surroundings, despite what Sir Stuffy Balls might imply.

Her handmade drapery business had gone from strength to strength in only two years and she'd had to employ two machinists just to keep up with demand. But she also knew that if she was to keep her business growing, she'd have to get more clients like Lord and Lady Tate-Fitzpatrick. No, she could not allow anything to sabotage this contract – least of all her apparent overwhelming lust for a rude older gentleman. She snorted at the word; he was the least gentle man she'd ever come in contact with. Heat spread suddenly and ferociously between her thighs as she created a mental image of what this ungentle man might do to her. *Fuck's sake.*

She grabbed the heavy sample book and slammed the tiny boot shut. There was room for the book and only the book in there, and Zoe clung on the thought that that was a good thing. The more space you have, the more you fill it, she told herself. She took a deep breath and filled her lungs with the air of the first crisp, earthy days of autumn. Looking down at her nipples, which were still erect, she reasoned that anyone would simply assume it was rather chilly outside, despite the heat rising from her glowing cheeks.

Perching the sample book on her forearm she opened the front door and went back into the hallway. Checking quickly, she was relieved when she saw nobody lurking and continued on to the far end. About halfway she was stopped by the looming figure of Lord Tate-Fitzpatrick, who seemed to appear from nowhere.

'Tell me something,' he said in a low gravelly tone that sounded worn by years of decadent living. Zoe forced her eyes to meet his.

'Yes?' she said flicking her gaze to her sample book to imply that she had business to attend to.

'Why are you here,' he said, even more quietly, and leaned in so that Zoe could feel his breath on her neck, 'measuring up *my* windows in *my* house wearing heels and stockings?'

Zoe gasped. 'I ... I beg your pardon?' she spluttered, backing away from him.

'You heard me.'

Suddenly furious, Zoe squared up to him, leaned towards him carefully and tried to match his tone. 'I will wear whatever the *fuck* I want to wear whenever I want to wear it.'

His expression softened and he seemed amused. He smiled and opened his palm to show her the way back to the room where Lady Tate-Fitzpatrick and her friend were waiting. Zoe nodded stiffly to him once and walked off in that direction. She was rather pleased with herself but realised the exchange had left her feeling even more turned on. How did he guess she was wearing stockings? She'd worn a pencil skirt with a good lining and checked every angle she could to make sure the snappers and suspenders were invisible. He must have a trained eye. Another bubble of excitement broke free from the knot in her chest and travelled down low into her panties, just at the point where, if she let them, her naked inner thighs rubbed together at the top of her stockings. She stopped just short of the door and squeezed her legs together, savouring the fact that the sticky dampness of her arousal had seeped out a little, coating her flesh with its naughty secret.

She'd worn the stockings knowing full well she'd be up and down ladders with a pencil behind her ear, measuring tape round her neck and a notebook between her teeth. It was nothing to do with being saucy – it was a tip her mother had given her many years before: 'It is impossible to appear unladylike when one is wearing a pair of good stockings.' And so, whenever she was meeting a client and poise and elegance were important, that's exactly what she wore. It hadn't occurred to her that something else might be implied by wearing such garments. The heady thrill of his breath tickling her neck was overriding her sensible side. She had to regain her composure. Counting back from three she turned the handle and smiled breezily at the women, who were poring over the glossy images in the magazines.

Zoe quickly became absorbed in showing the luscious fabric samples, matching swatches with the wallpaper and furniture. After they'd exhausted every combination and the conversation was beginning to turn to costs, a sharp knock at the door grabbed their attention and Lord Tate-Fitzpatrick cocked his head round for the second time.

'When you're done in here, I should like a consultation for new drapes in my billiard room,' he stated then closed the door.

Lady Tate-Fitzpatrick and her friend exchanged looks and raised eyebrows.

'Look out, you'll be tied face-down on the cloth and spanked before you know it,' the Lady said quite matter-of-factly.

'What?' Could this day get any more shocking? thought Zoe, but the Lady's words brought a renewed vigour to the arousal in Zoe's pussy and she wriggled in her seat.

'Oh, he doesn't want new curtains,' the Lady said, pulling a cigarette elegantly from a silver case and tapping it lightly. 'He just wants a quick fling. You'd better go quickly. He doesn't like to be kept waiting'

Zoe was confused. Was this woman giving her permission to fuck her husband?

'I don't understand,' she said while packing up her samples. 'You approve of his behaviour?'

'Approve?' She threw her head back and laughed in a shrill upper-class kind of way. 'I absolutely encourage it! That way, he does his thing, I do mine.' She winked at her friend. 'Don't I, Hilary?'

'Well, thank you for your time today, ladies. I will have a price for you in a couple of days.' And feeling very disarmed, Zoe made for the door, keen to get out of this strange kinky place and back to the safety of her scandal-free straight little life. She crept down the hall as silently as she could but was predictably met by Lord Tate-Fitzpatrick, who opened a door the second she walked past it.

'Took your time, didn't you? Right in here,' he said. So she followed him.

The room was panelled with dark wood, beautifully maintained, and had lush, thick shag carpeting. It was dim despite the sunny day outside – must be on the north side of the house, thought Zoe as she took in the rest of her surroundings. She almost smirked at the clichéd decor. There was even a faded globe, which probably doubled as a bar.

A bead of sweat formed at the nape of Zoe's neck and trickled down between her shoulder blades as she walked past the snooker table in the middle of the room. The image that Lady Tate-Fitzpatrick had conjured seared itself into Zoe's mind's eye and she rubbed her wrists at the thought of being restrained and dishevelled across such a mighty table. She shook the image from her brain and continued to the window.

'Just a simple replacement, is it?' she stated as evenly as she could, while putting down her sample book and getting out her measuring tape and pencil. Lord Tate-Fitzpatrick loomed up behind her, reached for the heavy, worn fabric, pulled the curtains together and plunged them both into darkness.

'Actually, I think they seem to work perfectly well, don't you?'

Zoe held her breath and stood completely still, wondering whether she should answer him. He was now close in behind her and suddenly both of his hands were on her hips, pulling her back towards his body. He slowly swayed her from side to side, rubbing his hard-on into her bottom. Her pussy clenched as he dipped his head into her hair and breathed in her scent. His hands crept further round to her abdomen, clutched her into him, explored her. Spreading out his fingers, he smoothed them down her skirt towards her mound, pulling the fabric taut to reveal her shape.

'My God,' he murmured into her hairline and the musky smell of him made her mouth water, but still she stayed absolutely still. His hands roamed up to her waist-band, reached in and freed her blouse to make room for his fingertips to feel their way over the fluttering flesh of her belly and up to her bra. Bending his knees behind her, he scooped both breasts into his hands and rolled his thumbs languidly about her nipples. She melted into him, let her head fall back onto his shoulder and swayed in time with his slow hypnotic movements.

He hooked his fingers into the lacy fabric of her bra, pulled it down and let her breasts fall out. The flighty material of her blouse danced over her freed flesh, raising goose bumps all over her body. She allowed herself to breathe more deeply and he must have sensed the shift as he began to nibble and kiss her neck, groaning all the while. Zoe pressed back into him, rubbing herself into his hard cock like a cat in heat. Her pussy felt slick and swollen with want and she willed him to reach down and pull up her skirt. Sliding her heels apart and grinding more forcefully onto him, she tried to get the hem to ride up of its own accord. Then suddenly he stopped, leaving her there panting in the darkness.

Once again she was wrong-footed. The arousal in her clit, which was at peaking point just seconds before, began to subside, leaving humiliation in its wake. What was he doing? She reached out her arms like a flailing blind person, feeling like a fool. Just as she was about to shout out in fury, static prickled in the room and the long lamps above the snooker table flickered on, their eerie mournful glow illuminating what seemed like acres of green baize.

'Where's the pockets?' she asked, then shivered at the sound of her voice breaking the electric spell.

'It's a billiard table' was the only explanation he gave. She was glad. She didn't actually want an answer, she didn't care, her pussy was on fire and she felt feral with desire. She began to rub her mound on the edge of the billiard table to try and get some relief.

'That's enough.' He stilled her by placing the flat of his palm on her buttocks. 'Now here's what we're going to do.' He spoke calmly with authority while sliding his hand up her back to her neck and bending her over the vast green expanse. 'I am going to tie you to this fine table and spank you.' Lady TP hadn't been wrong. Zoe smiled inwardly and a current of excitement travelled from her already tingling ass up to her nipples. 'All right?'

Zoe said nothing, thinking it a rhetorical question, but he persisted. 'I said, "All right?"'

Zoe realised he was seeking her permission.

'All right,' she purred, nestling her breasts and face into the cloth.

'Good.' And with that he reached round under her, grabbed her blouse and pulled it apart, tearing off the buttons. It was about the horniest thing that had ever happened to her and she was pleased that her breasts had remained outside her bra and her nipples now grazed the table. It was divine. She felt naughty and wicked but also immensely liberated. Even as he wrapped the golden-tassled curtain ties around each wrist and pulled tight, she felt freer than she ever had. She soared on the edge of her want and splayed her legs as best she could in her tight skirt, in invitation to Lord Tate-Fitzpatrick. At last she was secured to his satisfaction, long ropes taut against the green, and he took his position behind and slightly to the left of her. Bracing herself and holding her breath, Zoe squirmed as a droplet of moisture trickled into her already sodden panties.

Time seemed to span a lifetime as Zoe sensed him lift his arm into the air and pause. Dust motes stilled in the charged atmosphere for a moment then swirled into oblivion as his open palm smacked her hard through her skirt and panties. She rocked forward, jarring against the mahogany and slate. A rush of adrenalin seared through her as he took aim for the next. *Smack, smack, smack!* in quick succession in three different places.

'Pull up my skirt!' Zoe shrieked, shocking herself. Everything stopped and the Lord leaned over the table, his mass daunting and exciting, crushing her deeper into the barely cushioned slate.

'Excuse me?' he hissed, as if he was about to resist her demand, but his hand trailed down the back of her thigh to where her hem dug in from her trying to spread her legs.

'I said, pull up my fucking skirt.' She didn't know why but her utter arousal had brought with it a heady rage that made her feel feral and wanton and she didn't care.

'As the lady wishes,' he whispered and the warmth of his breath lingered as he left to take his position immediately behind her. She relaxed her stance to allow his hands access to the hem and he gripped it tightly. A squeal leapt from her throat as she realised that he absolutely was not going to pull her skirt up. He was going to pull it apart. And he did. With a roar he ripped the garment all the way to the waistband. Zoe was wet beyond belief as she imagined the scene he must be witnessing. She willed him to pull her knickers down over her buttocks and, just as she thought it, he did it. Pressing her toes into the ground, she raised her heels to give him the very best vantage point and held still for the next round of spanking. It came. She heard the first slap of flesh on flesh before she felt the sting. Oh, and the sting! Every muscle and sinew tensed as he administered smack upon smack to her exposed rump. Just when she thought she couldn't take any more, she realised he was whispering something over and over.

'Relax, just relax.' His voice was hypnotic and she began to let herself drop into the sound of it, while somewhere in the distance the smacking continued, pulling her out of herself into an inferno of heat and raw arousal. 'That's it, that's it ...' A new rhythm to ride on, over

71

and over. Her mouth was gaping and wet, hungry with the need to suckle something just as her pussy clenched and reached to his fingers. The smacking slowed and his palm lingered for seconds at a time on her searing flesh. Sometimes a fingertip trailed into her wet, hot slit. She bucked towards it, pulling on her restraints, beginning to tense up again and come back into her body.

He stopped smacking altogether now and calmed her by smoothing one hand up her back and into her hair, massaging her scalp while rubbing her bottom with the other hand. Every nerve ending was connected; she could see that now as her hair tingled. He slowly slid two fingers into her mouth and groaned as she took them deep into her, daring him to do the same in her pussy. He did, sliding his fingers forcibly into her desperate cunt while she suckled. She undulated her hips as he fucked her harder, swapping his fingers for his thumb so he could reach down to her aching clit, which was burning and ready for release. She closed her eyes tight and focused on that tiny nub that would soon take her over. Then he withdrew, from both her mouth and her pussy. She felt empty, hollow. Writhing and spreading herself as wide as she could, she begged him with her every move to fill her up again.

'I can see you might need a lesson in patience,' he said, wandering slowly to the other end of the table then dipping down as if to cue up a shot. His face was wickedly handsome and he smiled as his eyes raked his creation. 'You look magnificent, tied up like this. Though I think you may be a little free for my liking. A little too easy to get to.' Zoe stared at him and hoped her eyes conveyed her fury at being left on the brink of the horniest orgasm she'd ever had. Her arousal was ebbing away, leaving her pussy hot and twitching. The only thing that kept her from demanding to be released was curiosity. What would he do to her next?

He rose and disappeared into the darkness beyond the billiard table. Zoe could just make out the long shafts of cues lined up along one side, and she shivered as she saw his shadowy figure walk past them. And then he was back behind her, crouching low. He briefly trailed his stubbly jaw across the tender flesh on her buttocks and she winced, wondering if he would dive his tongue into her juicy lips. He didn't. He grabbed each ankle and roughly pulled her feet together. Zoe thought she heard a snapping of fabric or a belt and shivered with the delicious terror of not knowing what was going on.

Something was being wound around her ankles, then calves, not too tight, but enough to mean business. It felt like strapping or thick bands of fabric, almost like a bandage. It was being wound and wound all the way up, getting a little tighter each time until she felt like she was being made into some sort of dry-land mermaid. He stopped just below the crease of her buttocks and secured the strap. Now Zoe was completely stuck. She liked it. She liked the way he now began to massage her bum with strong long fingers, coaxing her arousal into play once more. She was glad to be at his mercy and, when he pressed against her and she felt his hard-on rage through his trousers, she was glad to be the one causing it.

He rubbed harder now, squeezing together then parting her fleshy buttocks rudely to reveal a sight that Zoe could only imagine. And she did: she put herself in his place, staring down at her swollen red cunt begging to be filled, and she moaned as he slid one of those sexy long digits right into it. She clenched tight, trying to hold it there, but her juices were flowing and he easily escaped her grip. This time she was rewarded with two fingers. She was amazed how easily accessible she was despite her bonds.

'You look so good, so ready,' he murmured, still working her.

'I am ready,' she purred back, hoping that, if he was looking for her permission to fuck her, he knew he had it.

And then she heard the clink and slide of a buckle being undone and a belt slid from its loops. Zoe braced herself for the sting of leather on flesh but relaxed as she heard it drop to the floor along with his trousers. Looping her fingers around her ropes, Zoe pulled tight, making her mound jar against the table, sending little shock waves into her clit, just as he spread her ass cheeks wide and plunged his cock right into her. He withdrew and immediately slammed hard again, then again, giving her no time to catch her breath. She was exhilarated and – astonishingly with no direct pressure on her clit – began to feel the well and rise from deep within her ravished pussy. It built to such intensity that she was terrified he might stop or change rhythm, so she had to scream out, 'Don't fucking stop!'

And he didn't. If anything he gained momentum and her pussy began to writhe and spasm, the pleasure mounting until Zoe couldn't hold on any more and let out a yell as she climaxed all over the achingly hard cock that was buried deep inside her. Two more thrusts and she felt the unmistakable shudder and still of the Lord coming right into her very depths. He collapsed on top of her and they breathed hard together until everything slowed and Zoe couldn't bear the crushing weight of him on her ribcage any longer.

'I can't breathe,' she whispered and he lifted off her with a quiet apology. He began to untie the strapping at her thighs, slowly rubbing where it had dug in, reviving the places where her legs had numbed. He was so gentle and quiet, nothing like the man who had brought her in here. He loosened the far end of her wrist restraints, slowly untied them and rubbed and soothed just as he had with her legs. He helped her off the table to stand up.

'I'm sorry about your blouse and skirt,' he said almost meekly but managed to look Zoe shyly in the eye. 'I seem to have ruined them.'

Zoe smiled at him and watched the relief flood into his expression. 'It was worth it,' she said and he grinned with a flash of the previous wickedness in it.

'Yes, yes, it was, rather.'

* * *

Wrapped in one of his silk smoking jackets, Zoe smiled up at the looming figure leaning into her tiny car. 'Now about my curtains,' said Lord TP with a very serious look. 'I'm disappointed about your lack of professionalism, Ms Lake.'

Zoe bit her lip. 'Customer satisfaction is my greatest concern, sir. Would you like me to make another appointment?'

'Yes.' His voice remained steely but his expression softened, cheeky almost. 'Yes, I would like that very much.'

Zoe resisted the temptation to wave, but as she drove off she stared in the rear-view mirror at Lord TP, who had the most glorious grin plastered upon his rugged face, as he waved her spoiled skirt above his head.

Beginner's Luck
Annabeth Leong

The sharply dressed instructor told everyone in the arm-binder class to take out a piece of rope. Rachel glanced around in confusion. She'd been to several kinky conferences with her ex, and rope bottoms such as herself got tied up by other people. She'd never been asked to do any tying before.

The command sank into the room slowly. Most people weren't awake for the first session of the day. They still sipped hotel coffee, shifted in narrow chairs and fiddled with rope bags piled on conference tables that had been shoved aside to make room for the hands-on class. The bottoms were having particular trouble understanding why they should look for rope rather than simply present themselves to their tops as a set of lovely, sexually responsive canvases. Even the muscular man to Rachel's right seemed uncertain – he probably wondered why he should bother doing anything with rope besides use it to wrap whatever willowy beauty currently swooned within his very capable arms.

Rachel made eye contact with a blonde across the room who had pinned up her long hair with a set of paperclips and a plastic ruler. The schoolteacher fantasy she inspired made Rachel grin. Unfortunately, the blonde didn't have any rope of her own. The women who attracted Rachel always seemed to be bottoms.

The instructor clapped his hands sharply. 'Bottoms, you, too,' he said, his voice snapping out like a drill sergeant's. 'I want you to understand exactly what your top is going to do to you. We are all going to go over these preliminary knots together.'

Rachel, unlike most of the other bottoms, actually did have her own rope and safety scissors, both brand-new and tucked into her favourite purple gym bag. When she'd decided to take the plunge and attend a kinky conference on her own for the first time, it had seemed an important part of her new-found sexual independence to bring her own equipment. She liked to be prepared.

She'd dressed tougher than usual for the occasion, too, putting on a thin black tank, skinny jeans and black heeled boots. She'd wanted to look exciting enough to live up to her red hair, like the sort of person who is always ready for adventure with a sexy stranger.

Rachel's hands trembled a little as she unzipped the gym bag. She lifted out a length of hemp, wrinkling her nose at the seaweed odour of the purple dye she'd used to colour it.

'Hey,' said the man to her right. 'Can I borrow some of that?' His big smile crinkled his cheeks. Rachel liked him immediately.

'You don't mind that it's purple?' She craned her neck, hoping for a look at his name tag.

'Beggars can't be choosers.' Melted caramel eyes almost distracted her from his biceps – but not quite. She smiled back and handed over a length of rope, barely restraining her sigh of disappointment when he turned to take it from her and she saw he'd circled 'bottom' on his name tag.

It didn't matter that this gorgeous, built blond man's name was Jeremy, or that he was indeed single, if he only wanted a woman who would top him. True, she'd never tried topping, but mastering complex knots seemed like a lot of work compared with her customary bottom role of relaxing in the blissful hold of a web of hemp. Rachel had listened plenty of times to the complex directions the instructors gave in these workshops, and wondered how her ex could possibly manage it.

Jeremy's smile turned flirtatious, and Rachel remembered she'd refused to fill out any of the information on her own tag besides her name. She'd wanted to leave things open for herself in her new-found freedom as a single woman, though the idea didn't make as much sense now as it had at the registration desk. Jeremy probably thought she was a top because she'd brought her own rope. She returned her attention to the instructor before he could say anything else.

'Just take this step by step and you'll definitely get it,' the instructor was saying. Rachel watched his fingers manipulate the length of rope in his hands. 'This is just a simple handcuff. It's quick to tie and easy to use. It won't stay on a bottom who's trying to wriggle out, but in a few minutes I'll show you how you can build a full arm-binder based on this one knot.'

Rachel imitated his movements, furrowing her brow a little and sticking her tongue into the corner of her mouth for concentration. Moments later, she held a beautiful pair of rope handcuffs.

She waited for the rest of the class to catch up, idly fantasising about the hot man next to her whipping a pair of these onto her, his big arms wrapping her even more securely than the rope while the stubble along his jaw tickled the side of her face. Too bad that fantasy wasn't realistic. She dismissed the thought and focused on the next task set by the instructor.

'Do you stick your tongue out like that while you're tying your submissives?' Jeremy asked.

Rachel shot him a look.

'It's adorable now, but I imagine it could be quite terrifying given the right circumstances. You're very good at this, obviously.'

Startled, Rachel glanced down at the neat pile of knots in her lap and for the first time compared her collection to the snarled tangles other people held. Warm pleasure suffused her chest. 'Thanks.' They grinned at each other for a second before she remembered herself. 'Look, I don't want to give you the wrong impression. I'm not actually a top.'

'Oh.' His face fell faster than a failed soufflé. Rachel instantly regretted her pronouncement. Was she sure she couldn't make an exception for a man this hot?

Jeremy gathered himself. 'That's fine,' he said. 'I mean, I understand. Not that I wouldn't have liked it if –' The big smile turned rueful. 'Women were very excited about me when I showed up at the conference on a motorcycle wearing a black leather jacket. That wore off pretty fast once I started revealing my preference. I expected to find more dominant women here, but they all seem taken.'

'I'm sorry.'

'Don't be.' He shrugged, clearly wanting to be gallant about his disappointment. 'I'm sure there's someone here for me.'

Just then, the instructor stashed his demo rope and clapped his hands again. '*Now* you can partner up,' he said.

'Good luck,' Rachel told Jeremy, and started her own scan of the room. She'd made friends at this conference in the past, and thought maybe one of them might like to play. Being tied up at a workshop seemed like a good icebreaker that might lead to hotter action in her hotel room later. Rachel had promised herself she would take charge here and get her needs met.

'Red! Over here!' A tall top waved at Rachel. She'd seen him teaching classes at the conference before. She shivered a little, remembering the time she'd watched him put a bottom in a hogtie and slowly tighten it until she gasped with helpless pain and arousal. He would do.

Rachel turned to say goodbye to Jeremy, and found him standing forlornly as a woman approached him with a grin only to turn her back the moment she got close enough to read his name tag. He'd crossed his arms over his chest in a way that emphasised the perfection of his pectorals, and Rachel wondered again about making an exception for him.

She glanced back at the tall top, who raised an eyebrow at her. She had competition for him, from an elegant brunette as well as the schoolteacher blonde she'd noticed at the start of class. He gestured for Rachel to hurry.

Jeremy was rejected twice more while Rachel hesitated. Were all these other women crazy? Who wouldn't go for that?

Rachel finally noticed the contradiction in her own brain and made a quick decision. She shrugged at the tall top, gestured toward his two other admirers, then tapped Jeremy on the shoulder.

He brightened for a second, then returned to being down-cast. 'I'm not a switch,' he said. 'And I'm no good at tying, myself. You saw what a mess I was making of the rope. But I can't believe you can't find someone who wants to top you. You're gorgeous. The men here can't all be blind.'

Rachel took a deep breath. 'I want to do you.'

'Huh? But you just told me –'

'I want to take a walk on the flip side,' Rachel said, surprised at how sharp her voice sounded, and at the heavy pounding in her chest.

'I don't need you to do me a favour.'

She let him see her gaze travel up and down his well-built body. 'I'm not. I'm doing myself one. Now, are you going to enjoy it, or not?'

A slow smile spread across his face – even his teeth were perfect. 'Yes, ma'am,' Jeremy said.

'Great.' Rachel retrieved her safety scissors and several lengths of rope from her bag. She steered Jeremy to face away from her, and angled him so that even around Jeremy's big arms she had a view of the instructor's demo bottom.

'Standard conference safeword applies,' the instructor was saying. 'If you don't like what your partner is doing to you, say "red". That goes for bottoms *and* tops.'

Rachel paused for a second with one hand on Jeremy's hard biceps. 'Do you mind if I play with you a little? More than just putting on the tie?'

'May I take off my shirt?'

'Please.'

Jeremy winked back at Rachel, then lifted the fabric off his torso, unveiling all the back definition she could have hoped for, along with a wave of spicy cinnamon rum cologne. Rachel caught her breath.

She didn't allow herself too much of a reverie, because she wanted to get started on the reality of him. She unwound her first length of rope and dragged it across his naked back while she waited for the instructor to begin.

Jeremy sucked in a breath. She pressed the rope a little harder into his flesh, massaging him with it and making sure the fibres scratched him. 'You like feeling it bite, don't you? Knowing that pretty soon it'll be clinging to your skin in a way you can't escape?'

'Yeah ...'

Rachel blinked in surprise at the dreamy tone of Jeremy's voice. It made sense, of course, that at least some of the things she liked about rope would appeal to another bottom, but it had never occurred to her that this would help her to top effectively.

Confidence surged through her. She started the armbinder by wrapping his body at armpit level, exhaling hotly against his neck as she dragged the hemp across his nipples on its way around his chest. She tied the starter knot the instructor showed, positioning it over his spine, but made sure to adjust the loop of rope several unnecessary times, just to scratch Jeremy's nipples some more.

'Oh, my God, you're evil,' he breathed. 'What are you doing to me?'

'Just what I like done to myself,' she said sweetly, then yanked at the encircling loop to get his attention. 'Now be quiet. You're distracting me. Put your hands behind your back so I can get this sleeve going.'

Jeremy moaned a little as he obeyed. Rachel smiled to herself.

She followed the interlacing pattern that would bind his arms together behind his back, pleased to discover that the knots she had to tie matched the pattern she'd woven in her lap moments before – the only difference was that now they contained Jeremy. They came easily to her, as if she'd learned them long ago, and Rachel reflected that she must have picked up more than she thought at those previous conferences.

Having the technical aspect figured out for the moment, she could concentrate on enjoying him. Rachel copped feels of his back muscles as she wound a series of loops around his arms that would eventually stretch from armpits to wrists. She tugged hard as she tied, forcing his body to sway from one side to the other in a rhythm she determined, and providing her with plenty of opportunities to place a steadying hand over his cut abs or at the base of the bulge of his biceps. She stroked him as she worked and murmured encouragements – she'd always preferred her top to interact with her while he tied her.

Getting bolder, Rachel rested a hand on the firm curve of Jeremy's ass while checking the tension of her most recent knot.

'Oh, come on,' Jeremy teased. 'You're not going to try to pretend you have to touch me there, too, are you?'

'It *is* necessary,' Rachel argued, laughing. 'I have to make sure you don't get bored.'

'Believe me, I'm not bored.' Jeremy gave a subtle thrust of his hips. Rachel rested her cheek against his biceps as she peered around him to look. Indeed, a thick bulge strained the front of his jeans. 'I haven't been this entertained in years,' he said. 'Are you sure you've never topped before?'

'Beginner's luck,' she said. 'Now, quiet, or I really will have to do something about the way you're distracting me.' She gave his ass a threatening promise of a squeeze, listening for the submissive sigh that let her know she'd got to him successfully.

She wanted to work her hand down the front of his jeans and feel that bulge, and had to forcibly remind herself they weren't alone. She bit her lip. How bad could it be to do that at a kinky event? Couples all around her in the repurposed conference room were earning mock-serious glares from the instructor every time they burst into brief flurries of slapping or moaning.

Rachel had never been comfortable with losing control in front of a room full of people, but a wild sensation rose in her chest. How could she lose control? She had control right now – over gorgeous Jeremy as well as over what they would do together.

She could not resist the temptation of the idea. She glanced from right to left. Even with her teasing, she'd completed the tie much more efficiently than most of the other tops. With the exception of the tall top – who had begun an extended improvisation involving artfully arranged twists of paracord and the elegant brunette's light brown nipples – they stared helplessly at tangled ropes, waiting for their turn to troubleshoot with the instructor. Their bottoms gazed with thinly veiled longing at the tall top.

The schoolteacher blonde had taken off her blouse and bra for the exercise, but her partner seemed oblivious to the sugared pink beauty of her bare nipples, cursing at the ropes snarled around her and tugging at them. The blonde rolled her eyes and shifted from one foot to the other.

Rachel imagined the splendid blonde also at her mercy, perhaps tied to keep those nipples pushed forward and available to Rachel's mouth. Then she straightened with a shock. She wasn't simply making an exception so she could get her hands on Jeremy's muscular physique, or even enjoying the empowerment of her new-found skill with rope. Sometime in the last 25 minutes, she'd gotten truly and torrentially wet, because topping really turned her on.

She had never questioned her ex's assumption that she would be the bottom, and she'd liked that enough to continue pursuing kink on her own. But no previous thrill compared to the high of a bottom hanging on her every gesture and longing for the strict touch of her hand. Rachel felt invincible, and ready for much more.

Rachel had caught Jeremy's attention. Could she secure the blonde's, too? A heady, reckless rush drove Rachel to catch her eye. She wound her right hand through the taut strands of rope holding Jeremy's arms behind his back and gently pulled him off balance, forcing him to lean against her for support and displaying him to the other woman.

Rachel ran a tickling finger through the trail of hairs leading to the button at the top of Jeremy's fly. He gasped and jerked, but she shushed him. 'You certainly look strong. All these muscles.' She licked the skin above his left trapezoid for emphasis. 'Why don't we find out how strong you are? Do you think you're strong enough to hold absolutely still and not make any noise while I do something to you?'

'What are you going to do?'

'What are you afraid I'll do?' Rachel whispered, and slid her hand into his jeans, right where it wanted to go. His cock greeted her fingertips with a slick welcome of pre-come and a hard shaft ridged with veins. Rachel closed her fingers around it and nudged his foreskin up and down over his cockhead, very, very slowly.

Jeremy let out a broken moan and nearly lost his balance. Rachel stabilised him, holding the arm-binder tight and making sure he leaned steadily across her shoulder. 'I would make you suck that,' she mouthed to the blonde, nodding toward Jeremy's groin. The other woman grinned and shook her body in an exaggerated tremor of arousal that confused her distracted top.

Rachel winked, feeling victorious, and returned her focus to Jeremy. Whatever games she played with the blonde, she didn't want to short-change her current captive. Rachel slipped her hand out of his pants and hoisted him into a standing position. 'I think I like seeing all that strength fail because of little old me,' she told him. He rewarded her with an ardent glance over his shoulder.

She ran her fingers down the sides of his arms and torso, grinning at his ticklish jerks. He looked good in her purple rope, she decided. She liked the sight of his intense masculinity trapped within her very feminine cage.

'How are you doing?' she murmured, checking the points of contact between the rope and his arm.

'Good,' Jeremy said. 'Really good. Thank you.'

Rachel rested her fingers in his palm. 'Squeeze my hand,' she said, testing his grip to make sure she hadn't pinched a nerve when she tied him. He responded with strength. 'Nice. Good job.'

'Do you have plans for the rest of the event?' Jeremy sighed.

'I think so,' Rachel said. Seeing the disappointed drop in his shoulders, she clarified. 'I think they involve you.'

She grabbed a spare length of rope and dragged it across the web tied around Jeremy's arms, making the entire lattice sing and buzz. The aching tremble of the rope passed into his body, then back through the rope and into her hands.

'I want to touch you so bad,' he said, punctuating the passion in his voice with a hard, visible swallow. 'I want to reach inside that little black tank top of yours.'

'That would be awful,' Rachel said, leaning forward to rub her chest against the side of his arm. Her nipples were so hard she was sure he could feel the tips of them even through her shirt. 'You see, I'm not wearing a bra.'

'I know,' Jeremy groaned. 'And I bet you have redhead nipples.'

'At least you're not asking me if the hair is natural.' Amused as she was, Rachel refrained from investigating the specifics of 'redhead nipples'. Instead, she gave the arm-binder another tug to remind Jeremy of her control. 'This is why we have to keep you tied up,' she said. 'A boy like you won't behave on his own.'

'No,' he agreed.

Rachel smiled and broke contact with him. The instructor was still working on his seemingly endless circuit of the room. He wouldn't have time to teach another tie – she could use the remaining fifteen minutes of class to whet Jeremy's appetite for things that might happen later.

Another scan of the room supported her assessment. The tall top and the brunette had absconded somewhere, probably to his hotel room, and many couples had given up on practising the arm-binder and were chatting softly with each other while toying with their ropes. Rachel considered following the tall top's lead and taking Jeremy out of there, but noticed the blonde's eyes on her again.

Rachel leaned forward and allowed her lips to brush Jeremy's ear. 'Do you see that blonde over there to the right? She has nice nipples, doesn't she?'

'Yeah.'

'Are they "blonde nipples?"' she teased. She took another moment to admire the pale pink standing out against the bare blue-white skin of her breasts.

'I think so,' Jeremy said.

'Do you know she's been watching us this whole class?'

'No. I was focused on what you were doing to me.'

'I'm glad to hear that, Jeremy. I'm glad you could be so focused. You're lucky, though, that I'm paying a little more attention.' She jerked the ropes again. 'I think maybe she wants to play with us. I was thinking about making a lunch date for the three of us, in my hotel room. Would you like that? Maybe I could tie the two of you together face to face and tell her to rub her blonde nipples all over this big chest of yours.'

'Rachel, I cannot figure out how you never discovered your dominant streak until now.'

She kissed the back of his neck. They both shivered, and she squeezed his ass. 'Maybe I needed the right bottom to motivate me to unleash myself.'

'Oh, God. I may not be enough of a masochist for all those puns.'

Rachel snorted. 'Fair enough. But tell me, Jeremy, do you want to invite her to play with us? In my room at lunchtime?'

'Hell, yes.'

'Then you'd better help me show her it'll be worth it.' Rachel punctuated her sentence by brushing her crotch across his bound hands. 'Of course, you're a gorgeous man. I want to tie you down and lick those washboard abs of yours until you can't stand it any more. I'm just not sure that'll be enough for her. She looks like she has high standards. I think you'd better show her you can do more than stand around looking pretty.'

'I'm good with my tongue,' Jeremy volunteered, and the associated flash of mental imagery broke the rolling dominant patter Rachel had managed to establish. She took a breath to steady herself, keeping him occupied by rubbing her crotch against his trapped fingers and plucking the taut loops that held him.

Rachel stood on her tiptoes to get as close to his ear as she could. 'That's nice to know for later, but at the moment I'm going to make myself come using your fingers. Right now. Right here.'

'In front of everyone?'

'In front of her.' She pressed another kiss to the side of his neck.

'Please do.' Jeremy wasted no time helping her, wriggling his hands within their bindings to find an angle that allowed him to undo the top button of Rachel's skinny jeans. She wiggled her hips to let him ease her zipper down, and gasped quietly when his fingers settled against the damp cloth of her underwear, barely separated from her clit.

Rachel braced herself with both hands on his rippling arm muscles. She liked feeling them struggle within the rope's constraints, contracting and releasing with Jeremy's effort to please her in spite of the bonds she had imposed.

'Make your fingers as stiff as your cock,' she whispered. 'And hold them still.'

'I wish you were rubbing against my cock right now.'

'Do a good job, and we'll see what happens.'

Rachel made eye contact with the blonde again, steering Jeremy to turn slightly to reveal the open flaps of fabric at the top of Rachel's jeans. Kissing the indent of flesh where the rope pulled Jeremy's shoulders together, Rachel leaned into him and embraced him. She knew the pleasure of being held and restrained like he was, but now she revelled in her discovery of how good it felt to hold him, to please herself using his body.

The blonde seemed riveted by the scene, staring openly. Rachel sighed and ground her hips against Jeremy's bound hands, floating on a fantasy of tying them both into this arm-binder, then weaving the two sets of rope together so Jeremy and the blonde were trapped back to back. After that, she would make them kneel and grind her clit against their mouths, first one and then the other, until she got tired of coming. Then she would allow them to pleasure each other until she was ready for more.

Rachel gasped and bit Jeremy's shoulder to silence her groan as she came. He grunted and absorbed her weight as she rested on him a moment, catching the last of her pleasure with rhythmic rubs against his hand.

'You'll get your turn, too,' she promised, pulling back and slipping her hands quickly between their bodies to fix her jeans. She glanced at the clock. Two more minutes until the end of class, and she felt sure the blonde would be headed their way.

Jeremy twisted his body as much as the arm-binder allowed, looking back at Rachel. 'So, have I converted you to a top?' he asked. 'Because, God, I hope so.'

Rachel pulled him into a quick but passionate kiss. 'Let's just say, I think the interlude we're about to have with that blonde is only the first of our adventures.'

Getting Somewhere
Maxine Marsh

As long as I could remember, I'd always had a thing for the sight of a man in a hat and leather boots – the kind worn on a horse, that is, not on a bike. Something about the drawl in their voices and the dust in the air, the sun and the smell of farms coming in through an open car window, seduced me without fail. I felt at home in those places. So when I graduated college a year early, completely uninterested in pursuing a job related to my major, I typed up my meagre résumé and sent it out to five ranches that I'd seen were hiring hands for the summer. I had a little experience with equines in the short year my dad had been stationed in the Lone Star state. By some sort of luck I'd landed a menial position at Barrett's Rehabilitation and Boarding, and found myself smack dab with two feet firmly on the ground in small-town Texas.

Excited to start out my life, I guess I had expectations about the type of men I'd find populating the place. Those expectations fizzled out when I discovered that the men my age here just weren't any different from those I'd come across before. Not the quiet and tough, silently intimidating men I'd craved; no one that made me feel beside myself with longing. After a couple of months at my new job, I sank myself into my work, happy to be around the horses and the countryside, figuring that whatever it was I needed just wasn't available.

After a few months, I forgot I was lonely. At least I thought I had. But that was before Mr Barrett, my boss, hit me.

He was making rounds in the middle of the afternoon when he came in and found me fiddling with a horse-whip. It was decorative, something left over from the real cowboy days, but the iron hook it had been mounted on had fallen off onto the floor of the barn.

'Gail.'

Mr Marshall Barrett was an intimidating man. He was tall and broad as a bull, but had some age on him, sporting neatly trimmed silver-streaked hair that clashed with his black eyes, like a storm brewing. He always seemed to be evaluating me. He was one of those old-school ranchers – quiet and disciplined, traditional in his love of ranching, hardworking and expecting everyone else to be just the same way. Being raised by a military father myself, I reacted to such expectation by doing my very best job, whether it was shovelling manure or dressing down the horses. Since I'd started at Mr Barrett's ranch, I'd felt that familiar itching of wanting him to be pleased with me, an embarrassing tendency, but one I couldn't much help.

'Mr Barrett, this fell.' I held the piece of iron, two loose screws and the attached whip out to him sheepishly.

He took it, then looked at the spot on the wall where it had been hanging. 'The holes gave. I'll find another spot for it,' he said.

He pulled at the whip, but it wouldn't come out of the little metal ring that the handle end had been set in. With those thick arms, which I could see bulging even underneath his long-sleeved work shirt, he pulled at it. The stubborn leather began to bend and loosen up as he applied more pull to the handle end just under the start of the whip strands. Suddenly, the whip came loose from its bond and Mr Barrett's hand flew back with it, sending the strands of rawhide leather straight across my right cheek.

I gasped, took a step back and put a hand to my cheek. A wretched burning flared from my jaw to my temple and after a few seconds began throbbing.

'Are you all right?' Mr Barrett asked with only the barest concern in his voice.

I wasn't sure I was, but like most people I answered on

autopilot. 'Yes.' I was able to make myself take my hand off the burning line buzzing across my skin. I wanted to get on with things, flee from the embarrassing incident, but I couldn't make my feet move.

'I'm sorry,' he said steadily.

I shrugged. 'No big deal, it was an accident.'

Still, I couldn't move. It was like my body had detached from my brain and was waiting for permission from him. How could it be that my body had interpreted the lash as some kind of command? My feet, my legs, the spot between them I refused to believe was involved in this coup, my torso, my breasts and the nipples aching against my bra, my arms and neck and head – all of it was standing at attention. For him. And I didn't know why.

He took a sudden step forward. I flinched. He ignored my reaction, looking closer at the offended cheek. 'Go to the office and put some ice on that. It'll help keep the swelling from getting too bad.'

Finally, I was able to move.

* * *

He came around the next day when I was tugging a bale of hay out to the feed station. I guess I'd been grimacing a bit because he stopped mid-step and asked, his voice low and burly, 'What's wrong, Gail?'

Seeing him brought a funny feeling to my gut. I wiped my brow and shook my head. 'Nothing, Mr Barrett. My shoulder's just sore is all.'

To my surprise, he reached out and took my shoulder in his hand. 'Why?' His hand was big enough to fit my shoulder in his palm. He squeezed it, poking his fingertips into the dips of sinewy tendon in my shoulder blade.

I winced a little before I could hide the discomfort. 'Just slept on it wrong, I guess.' It was a lie. I'd fallen a few days prior, catching myself straight down on my right hand and jamming my shoulder in the process. It ached whenever I moved something heavy.

He continued rubbing. My body went taut as I imagined his hand straying to other places too. I was embarrassed by that thought and looked away.

'Look at me,' he said brusquely.

I immediately did as he instructed. He prodded here and there in my shoulder blade, watching my eyes with an intensity that made me blush, the way he would if he was looking into a horse's eyes for signs of pain or discomfort.

'I don't think it's a serious injury. But you do need to stretch it out so it doesn't get stiff.'

I nodded, barely even hearing. I was too busy willing my body not to quiver.

'Come.'

He led me to a stall in the far corner of the barn. It was a large stall, set up to house equipment and keep extra bales and troughs out of the way, the kind of musty room most of the other hands avoided. I was instantly aware of how alone we were, of how the wooden slats in the wall let in little peeps of sunlight, striping the walls lined with hooks that held all sorts of tack.

He reached for some idle ropes.

'Stand here.'

I went to his side, near the wall, and waited while he took down a long rope and began to tie it to a thick iron hook above me. He was standing so close while tying the rope that the bulge of my breasts rubbed against his chest, sending an electric shock pulsing through my nipples and down to my crotch. It happened again as he shifted around, grabbed my right wrist and began to tie it to the rope hanging from the hook. I bit the inside of my lip to keep from moaning. Even then I don't think he realised what he did to me, standing so close and all. Or maybe he did and just didn't care. Either way, by the time he'd tied the rope securely above me, I'd become insanely aroused. I'd forgotten what it was like to feel so turned on, just from the proximity of another warm body.

'There,' he said, taking a step back to appraise the situation. My right wrist was tied up above my head so that my arm was fully extended. 'Now pull your weight down a bit, so your shoulder gets a proper stretch.'

100

I did as he said, sort of bending my knees until my arm was stretched taut, and I began to feel a heavenly pull in my shoulder. Looking up, I admired the steadfastness of the knot, the way it coiled around the iron hook and then around my wrist, firm but not uncomfortable. I let my weight down a little. It felt good, very good, but I soon realised that my position – back up against the wall, right arm straight up, my knees bending to increase my crouch – caused my breasts to push outwards, right at him. I'd slipped into a tight white tank top that morning, and now my cleavage was starting to pop up at the scoop neck. I was acutely aware of how exposed I felt. He just stood there right in front of me, arms crossed, watching.

I tried to tell myself that it was all in my head, that he was just trying to help me sort out this sore-shoulder business. But no matter how hard I fought in my mind to convince myself that this was all innocent, I couldn't help really feeling like I was on display for him. On display and at his mercy, being that I was tied up and all, those critical eyes of his evaluating me every second that passed. I squatted further down, sure that the hardening nubs at the tip of my breasts were completely visible through my shirt and bra. I was sure he could see them. I'd picked my thinnest white cotton bra and my lightest top, expecting the day to be hot. And I guessed I'd been right about that, just not in the way I'd expected.

'Do you have enough leverage?' he asked.

'I … I guess,' I stammered.

He came over and undid the rope. When I made to move away, he put a hand on my torso, pressing me back against the wall. I gasped, but he stood unmoved. 'Stay.'

He re-looped the rope, took up the extra slack and refastened my wrist to the screw hook again. This time, though, there was a good deal of extra length hanging from the knot around my wrist. He took the extra length, threaded it behind me and up through my legs, and then wrapped it once around another thick hook a few feet away on the wall on the other side of me. The way the rope was drawn up between my legs made it rub in the most indecent spot it possibly could. My mouth and my throat dried instantly, and I began to shake a little.

'Put your weight down,' he said.

I half-crouched down, knees knocking. He pulled on the rope, which added a nice amount of force to the stretch, but also had the unfortunate side-effect of digging right down into my crotch. My jeans were tight enough as it was, but now the seam between my legs was practically crushing my clitoris.

He began to pull and release a little, and then repeat, which sort of slowly pulled and released me, up and down, stretching and then relaxing my shoulder accordingly. I had been trying to hold my breath, hoping he'd think enough was enough and let me out of the precarious position, but as it went on and on, I could not stop myself panting at the exquisite feeling building between my legs. I bit my lip, trying to silence my growing arousal.

'Relax,' he said.

I did, which caused me to sink further down. Before I realised it, the aching knot of my clitoris burst loose. There I stood, shaking and moaning and coming up against the tack-room wall, while my boss watched.

As I caught my breath, he unwound the rope and threaded it back between my legs. He loosened the knot that was around my wrist but didn't untie me completely.

'You ought to be able to get yourself out of that,' he said before leaving me alone in the stall.

* * *

I was doing the last of the chores that night when Mr Barrett came in. He paused, looking at the wheelbarrow of manure I was hunched over and the shovel in my hand, and said, 'Finish up what you're doing. I need a word.'

'OK, Mr Barrett.'

He was sure to say something about this afternoon, about how disgusted he was with me, that he thought maybe I needed psychological help or something. So when I went to his office, I could only stand in front of his desk like a guilty little girl who had been summoned to the principal's office.

'Do you know why I keep you on, Gail?' He didn't even look up from his paperwork when he asked.

I was right. He was going to reprimand me. I thought about it. He had made many of the others' jobs temporary summer posts; the business just hadn't been coming in enough to keep so many hands on. I'd assumed I had only kept my position because of seniority – I'd started months earlier than most of the others and was one of the only employees who didn't have constraints to keep them from working late. My nightlife was nonexistent. But now maybe he was doubting his decision to keep me on.

'No, Mr Barrett.'

'Because you care. About your responsibilities, about the horses. Sometimes it's hard to get you kids to take your work seriously.'

Being called a kid didn't rub me the wrong way. Mr Barrett was probably close to fifty, and I'm sure we seemed like kids to him. Either way, I realised he was extending a rare bit of praise.

'I do my best,' I said.

'You put in extra effort, you stay late most nights. I've noticed. I need people who take care of their responsibilities.'

It was just my personality to make sure everything was neat and tidy before leaving each night but I also liked the calm of the stables at dusk when night was falling and the horses were settling. I could have sworn that they snorted to one another subtly, not talking, but communicating their presence to one another. I hadn't thought he'd really noticed, and I certainly hadn't done it to get noticed.

'Well, thank you, sir. I do love horses.'

He looked up at me and smiled. He was such a serious man, always so stern, that I didn't know if I'd ever seen him smile. I realised how handsome he was, how the smile reached his eyes and made him seem so sincere and warm. It made me feel safe and comfortable there in front of the man I'd been so fearful I had disappointed. The smile left and the steady sternness returned. I realised I was staring and looked away.

'*That* is why I keep you on. OK?'

I nodded, a little confused.

'Now come here.' He turned his chair.

My mind went quiet, my brain idled in neutral. I walked around his desk, stopped in front of him, waited to be told what to do. Whatever it was, I would do it – the smallest praise from him made me feel like such a good girl, and I wanted to feel that high again. He reached and grabbed my hand and pulled down on it so hard that I fell to my knees between his legs.

There was a moment of stillness, while he sat there, his eyes devouring me with such hungry confidence that I felt the entire universe focus down on me. Reasoning fuzzy, I reached for his crotch. Beneath my palm it felt warm and hard. My fingers found the fastening on his jeans and then the zipper, and when he lifted his hips up I managed to work his pants down around his thighs.

Oh, God, I could smell him. His musk after a day of subtle country sweat, mixed with the scent of faded denim, was mouth-watering. He smelled like a cowboy. A *real* cowboy.

I immediately dove onto his cock like I was starving for it. I was embarrassingly enthusiastic for a moment there.

His all-encompassing hands pressed at the back of my head as he urged me to slow down. Fortunately, with his entire cock stuffed into my eager mouth, I really didn't have a choice. I mapped the underside with my tongue and then pushed further forward, wanting every last bit of him inside my face. As soon as I'd gotten the tip of his exquisite cock to the back of my throat, Mr Barrett gently but firmly grabbed both of my hands and placed them on either armrest of his chair. I peeked up. He had overlapped my hands with his own, firmly enough that I knew he would not release them, even if I gave them a good tug. Being held down, both by his hands and his eyes, without the slightest sign of give, thrilled me. I went back to the task at hand, wondering if I had really done a good enough job around the ranch to deserve such a pleasure.

I was by no means an expert cocksucker, so I hoped

my enthusiasm would make up for whatever I lacked in the technique department. Since I didn't have use of my hands, I was concerned that my mouth would lose its grip on his cock. I made long, slow strokes up and down the entirety of his shaft while keeping the head in my mouth and then returned back down his shaft to the root. When I began to feel in control, I ventured to pull his cockhead out halfway from my lips, keeping it from popping out by applying generous suction.

He was as quiet as a country evening up there. The slight parting of his lips and the way he stroked my wrists with his fingertips, all the while holding me down tightly, indicated he was enjoying it just fine.

I moved in a rhythmic bobbing until I'd lulled myself into painful arousal. I fantasised about mounting him and thrusting my cunt up and down over his cock. My slit grew moist and I became lost in it, taken over until I writhed around, hoping to catch my clit on the seam of my jeans, savouring the weight of his palms squashed down hard over the backs of my hands, pumping my mouth over his cock like it was a pussy. I was so far gone, I moaned and whimpered like a complete slut around his girth, allowing my saliva to pool around my lips, loving the way it dripped down my chin in little strings.

He remained so quiet that the only clue I had of his impending climax was the jarring of his hips as they rose up and bucked toward me. When he came, he released my hands to grab my head and shoved my face over his lap as hard as he could, grunting as his hot semen poured from his body into mine. I swallowed around him, taking all of it in with innocent eagerness. He gave a heavy sigh when he finally let go of me.

I stood up on unsure feet, wiped my mouth and chin on my palms and pushed back behind my ears some errant wisps of hair that had come loose. As soon as I had finished rearranging myself, and he'd pulled up and refastened his jeans and tucked his shirt, a cold realisation of what I'd just done hit me.

I'd gotten down on my knees and sucked my boss off. Like some kind of mindless bimbo.

I just stood there the way I had the other day when he'd accidentally whipped me in the face. My body was keen, every sensitive bit of my flesh from my lips to my nipples, the drenched flesh between my legs, the soft spot on the heel of my foot that had always been an erogenous zone for me – all of it ready to be touched and tormented. Completely in contrast, my brain sizzled with acute shame, showing me disgraceful replays of what I'd just done.

'Are you all right?' he asked in that steady drawl of his. He remained seated authoritatively behind his desk like nothing out of the ordinary had just happened.

I was so mortified that I could only nod. He was sure to call me a hundred different variations of the word 'whore' and then fire me. And still my inner pussy muscles contracted in desperate need. I was like a mare in heat. I'd never been so swept away by impulse yet, amidst the swirling tumult of disgrace, I was undeniably turned on.

He said, 'Get home, Gail,' before turning back to the paperwork on his desk.

* * *

My home wasn't my little apartment in the little town a few miles away. My home was now the ranch. Realising this, aching for a particular place for the first time since I was a little girl, a time before I had learned not to get attached, was disarming. I'd been looking for this and found it, and now I wasn't sure I wanted it.

I went to work the next day and took a ride out on a horse named Hayward. He needed exercise and I needed to ride myself raw, out and away. Halfway out I put a hand down my jeans and humped my hand until my core melted. It was a superficial win. By the time I'd made it back to the stalls, the uneasy feeling was back. Mr Barrett was inside the stables, checking up on things, when I pulled Hayward in to rub him down and water him.

The way he watched me go about my chores told me he suspected what I'd been up to, and I spent most of the time trying not to let him see my furious blush, hoping the wetness between my legs wasn't seeping into view.

109

After I'd finished with Hayward, Mr Barrett approached me and said, 'I need you to stay late tonight, Gail. I have some work in the stables for you before you leave.'

'OK, Mr Barrett.'

He didn't come by until it was dark, and everyone else was gone. When he came in, he gestured for me to follow him and led me into a free stall toward the back of the stable.

'Stay here,' he said.

I waited and a minute later he was back with a chair and rope.

'Sit.'

I sat.

Without a word he wrapped the rope around my upper body, pulling it just tight enough to draw my back to the back of the chair. He criss-crossed the rope between my breasts and over my shoulders, and then around and under them so that my cleavage rose when he secured the rope in a knot behind me. With a second length of rope he made a similar pattern over my lap, encouraging me to raise each leg so that the rope crossed over one thigh and under the other, and then back around until they were tightened down fairly secure. When he'd finished, the bindings crossed and wound tightly up near my crotch, just enough to tease my sensitive bits. The pressure on my breasts was maddening, too.

Hypnotised by his motion, it didn't occur to me, until

he stood back and looked at the configuration he'd created, that Mr Barrett had done this before. Tied a girl up in a chair, probably just the same. How else would he know exactly how to tie me, which knots to make, what length of rope to use? He'd done this before, he's into *this* sort of thing. And then it occurred to me that although he was into this sort of thing, it was quite out of the ordinary for me. I started to pull against the rope, hoping it'd slip loose enough to let me escape. It didn't.

He frowned down at me.

'What? What did I do?' I kept struggling.

He crouched down, the way a parent would do when they wanted to have a serious talk with their little child. 'You need time to think, Gail. You really do.'

The way he sounded subtly exasperated with me made me want to cry, like I'd disappointed him. 'About what?'

'You seem all balled up inside, Gail. It's clear to see. There's a heap of discord you need to work through. Sit here quietly tonight, and decide what it is you want, or don't want. I'll come back when you've decided.'

With that he stood and left the stall and closed the door. The latch clicked into place, and his feet thumped on the floor as he walked away. He didn't even say how he'd know I was ready. He didn't even say! I started to panic.

'Mr Barrett, please! Come back! I don't want to sit here all night!'

No response, nothing but lights clicking off, and then silence.

'Marshall!'

I spent the next ten minutes hollering, at first for him, and then just hollering. I just felt this energy, sitting there in that little chair, surrounded by the hushful noises of the horses, by the smell of rugged life and hay. It made me just keep on hollering. I heard footsteps again and halted my yelling. The light in the barn came back on and he opened the stall door. Without so much as stopping to take a look at me, he knelt down, wrapped a bandana over my mouth and tied it tight behind my head.

When he was done, he stood back and looked at me. 'I said you are to sit here, *quietly*, and think. Hollerin' doesn't help you think, it helps you *not* think.'

With that sentiment, he left again.

* * *

I imagined him going down the back driveway to his house, getting ready for bed, taking off his clothes, maybe even sliding that massive body of his in between the cool sheets completely naked. Maybe he'd turn over onto his back, staring up at the dark ceiling but seeing other things. Maybe he would cup his balls, feel the skin tighten up and pull back, feel the stirrings of need. Without rushing he'd take his cock in his hand, draw his palm over it, up and down and around it, and sigh into the quiet of his bedroom. He'd jerk off in the night, undoubtedly pushed to the brink in minutes, knowing he had a girl tied up in the barn down the way, waiting, suffering his order to sit and think. And he would consider all the things he could do to me, knowing I was at the mercy of whatever it was that had developed between us, knowing I would give in to all of it.

I conveniently ignored the truth that he didn't want the control over me – he wanted me to hand it over, to be completely conscious of my acquiescence to him, to embrace it. Sitting there in the dark, I pushed any thought of that away. I accepted that I was seduced by him. But I still hadn't accepted whether or not I *wanted* to be. I managed hours of torturing sexual fantasy about him, without once asking myself why I was really tied up in his barn.

Hours later, he came in quietly. My eyes adjusted to the lights, revealing his imposing form over me, jaw set as sternly as it had been when he'd left. Without a word he unbuttoned his pants. The outline of his rigid cock in the glaring light was utterly divine. He took it in his hand right there in front of me and began stroking it. For a few seconds I was caught in the pull of his gaze while he not only looked at me but *saw* me too, until I felt a burn of submissive humiliation begin to pulse through my veins. He knew every one of the dirty fantasies I'd had, as sure as if I'd said them out loud.

His hand quickened, drawing my attention. I felt so strong a need to suck his cock, I could have cried.

'Have you decided?' he asked.

My mind was a mess, even as I tried to reason an answer to his question. Had I? It was hard to think with that noise – the fleshy noise his hand made as it flapped over his cock right in front of my face – echoing in my head over and over.

'Have you, Gail?' There was an urgency.

I felt a huge pit opening in my stomach, the fear swimming round and round. I shook my head; I couldn't decide. His features were a mixed battle of arousal and growing disappointment. He took some steps back and rested against the stall door as he jerked himself off furiously. His withdrawal from me made me feel twice as consumed, and I whimpered at him a little through the makeshift gag.

'What a shame.'

His eyes turned to slits as he neared his end, narrowed but locked on mine just the same. *Shame, shame, shame,* they said. He didn't tear his glare away from me for a second, not one second. No matter how desperate his need for release grew, he showed the desire to me openly and without a straw of hesitation. *What a shame.*

And then I found my way past it. I nodded hard, saying, 'Yes, yes, yes' through the bandana that had dried my tongue out. I wanted the shame, I wanted the cowboy to shame me, or I'd suffer a deeper, more painful sort of shame, the kind that wasn't nearly as pleasant. I desperately tilted the chair, thinking maybe I could hop over there before time ran out. I wanted his come in my mouth, over my face, mucking up my hair, more than I'd ever wanted anything in my life.

Mr Barrett must have been convinced, because he ripped the bandana off me, aimed his cock at my face and split open the night with a roar of orgasm that scared the horses. It was so intensely erotic that I felt my clit surge. Any stimulation to it would have set off my own climax, but I couldn't worry about that right away, because I was too busy sucking on his cock, slurping up the last remains of his release.

'That a girl,' he whispered, taking my head in his hands and gently urging his spent cock to the back of my throat, deeper, deeper, deeper. 'Now we're getting somewhere.'

OOPS!
Flora Dain

Like it's in slow motion, I watch spellbound as the tall porcelain cup tilts on my tray, slips over sideways and sends a warm gush of coffee all down his gleaming white shirt-front. It soaks his flies and spatters the financial journal he's reading.

This is a whipping offence.

'Oops!' I lean forward with a playful grin and flutter my eyelashes. My breasts, all size-40-double-D-worth, bulge temptingly over the rim of saucy white lace and brush his cheek as I bend over to mop up the mess.

I'm wearing my newest French maid's costume, the one with the cutaway front and the frilly apron that stops just short of my stocking tops and flutters away from my pink, exposed slit at the slightest movement.

'Accidents will happen,' I giggle and dab at his flies with a teeny hanky, clearly inadequate.

116

Another offence – a caning? 'Shall I get another cup, sir?'

He glances up.

Aha! A reaction. But not the one I expect.

Instead of a glint of fury or an explosion of temper he simply picks up a notepad and writes very clearly the number 8.

Oh, no. Not again. My heart sinks.

'OK.' He sighs and carries on reading.

He doesn't even look at me. And I've made a real effort tonight – full make-up, pouty expression, highest heels, tightest basque under my naughtiest maid's uniform – and he's barely noticed.

I finish dabbing, lingering a little over his flies in a suggestive sort of way, and brush his face with my breasts again. But he stares absently at the notepad and taps his pen against his chin as if I'm not even in the room.

I bend over his lap to reach the cup, now lying on the carpet. An ugly brown stain has soaked the fluffy white pile. I pose gracefully over his knees with my bottom high up almost under his nose and wait.

Nothing happens. I ease myself upright, summon what's left of my shredded dignity and flounce off to the kitchen to make another cup.

When I glance back he's looking thoughtfully at the mess on the carpet. He writes another number on the pad.

Grr. This is serious.

It's been going on a while now. I'm a nervous wreck.

I've never seen him like this before.

I don't know what to do.

* * *

We've been together nearly a year and we've fallen into a pretty regular routine, like any couple, I guess, except that for us it's a little more so. My partner is also my Dom.

I still come up in goose bumps when I think how we met.

I'd been playing around in some chat rooms before an evening out with some friends. He was sitting on the next table and quite by chance I'd brushed against him and automatically said, 'Sorry' before I realised who he was.

One of the senior partners. He was with friends too.

He looked up for an instant. He's really, really attractive – sort of tallish and distinguished looking.

I thought it would be *years* before we met – I'd only started that week as an office junior. And here he was, just inches away. The rest of the evening went by in a daze, until I got home and fired up my computer to check my email.

Suddenly this message popped up with my name on it – 'Cally?'

Who was this? I typed 'Hi' back and then 'It's very late. Have you been having a good time?'

Instantly the reply came back. 'I'd be having a better one with you over my knee, Calliope.'

He – or she – knew my real name.

I stared. Who *was* this?

Without stopping to think about the risk I was taking – that's how hyped up I was – I typed right back, 'Wow. Do I know you?'

Instantly a message ribboned across the screen. 'Not as well as you should. Shall we meet?'

'How do you know my name?'

'Come back to the Club and I'll tell you.'

So it was somebody there. They'd seen me.

And they wanted to spank me.

Wow. I mean, how could I resist? I hightailed it back to the Club, thinking it would be a waste of time. All my friends had gone home. How could I even walk in there on my own? It would look so – *brazen.*

Just then a man moved out of the shadows. And it was him – the sexy senior partner. My legs turned to jelly while he stood there like he'd stepped out of a movie poster.

He reached out a finger and drew it lightly across my cheek. 'You're very punctual, Calliope. I like that.'

Pow. I melted. From that second I was his, utterly and completely. But I did my best to seem unconcerned, knowing all the while that whatever he was going to ask me to do, I'd do, and fast.

Probably twice.

We went back into the Club and he ordered champagne. He talked to me quietly, his hand moving gently along my thigh. I could hardly keep still, I was so excited. He knew my name from my application form. When I looked surprised he murmured that all staff emails and online Internet searches are monitored and he'd found my search history very, *very* interesting.

My face burned as I recalled some of the hot bondage sites I'd looked at on my first day. The firm's Internet access is – how shall I put this? – very sophisticated. He even knew my passwords.

And come to think of it, every time I'd passed him in the corridor I'd blushed. Maybe he'd noticed that too.

After a while he took me back to his apartment. And before long I *was* over his knee, and I was getting the most severe spanking I'd ever had in my life, and when he'd done and I'd slithered to the floor emotionally exhausted from all the crying and laughing and wriggling about, he leaned down and kissed me on the mouth.

He kissed me like he was starving, a deep, full invasion, tongue to tongue, like he'd never tasted anything so good in his life. When he finally let me breathe he smiled down into my eyes and I melted all over again.

'We're going to be terrific together, Calliope. You're delicious.'

* * *

Needless to say, spanking wasn't all he wanted. After that first night, when he tied me to the bed and took me every which way and then some, we settled into a kind of routine. It soon became clear exactly what he liked.

He's very strict. What he likes is instant obedience. And if he doesn't get it he gets angry, period. And when he's angry … *wow*.

The first time it happened was our first morning. I'd tumbled out of bed, all tousled and bleary and a bit stiff from all the tying up, found the kitchen and made us both a cup of coffee. While it was brewing I'd sashayed round the kitchen, humming a little, dressed in his last-night's shirt I'd scooped up off the floor and admiring myself in the glossy surface of the cooker.

I looked pretty good, all wild hair and big eyes and wide, come-and-fuck-me-again smile.

'What are you doing?'

I jumped about a foot, spun round and knocked over one of the cups. It smashed on the granite worktop and coffee ran all down the pristine white laminate doors to the spotless white floor and oozed into a brown, tarry puddle.

He was leaning in the doorway watching and he looked gorgeous, all biceps, broad chest and mussed-up hair, like he'd just fought off a lion in the Colosseum.

I grinned back, feeling playful. 'What does it look like? I'm making coffee. And, um, spilling it.'

His face seemed to darken like thunder in the distance. 'Did you do that on purpose, Calliope?'

Whoa. He said it so softly I stared at him. A sort of smile was making the corner of his lips twitch, and his eyes were gleaming again, with a kind of weird glow that sent a surge of electricity straight through me.

I licked my lips and eyed him from under my lashes. 'Yes.'

His eyes narrowed. 'Good.'

Just that.

He walked into the kitchen, peeled his shirt off my back like it was a banana skin and fell on my mouth, hungry all over again, running his hands all over me, into places he'd explored in other ways and very energetically last night. And all the while his erection was beating its own rhythm against my belly like it would burn me up.

But instead of making me kneel in front of him there and then and take him in my mouth he pulled away with a groan and led me past the bedroom, past the living area, and opened a door in another part of the apartment I'd not seen before.

'This is my office. I do a lot of work here.' He tilted an eyebrow towards a desk, a computer and a fax machine at one side of the room. 'But the business end is over there.'

The other end was straight out of a porno, with a state-of-the-art spanking bench, rails, posts and a trapeze.

The rails held whips, paddles, two or three riding crops, floggers and a selection of scary masks.

I stood very still, taking it all in, and when I finally dragged my eyes back up to his face I saw he was eaten up with excitement. His eyes positively *danced*.

'When you make mistakes you'll come in here and we'll do something about them. Do you understand?'

I breathed out very slowly, not realising until that second how long I'd been holding my breath. 'Yes, sir.'

He smiled then, a grin of pure, animal satisfaction. He took my face in his hand and tilted up my chin, gave me a long, searching look and then touched his lips very lightly to my forehead. 'You have to want to improve, or there's no point. So you have to want to come here. Nothing happens in here unless you consent.'

I was already throbbing, moisture gathering between my legs. He sounded so damned *hot*.

The sight of all this stuff, and the thought of what this gorgeous man did in here, was overwhelming. I'd dreamed about it, I'd seen pictures of it, I'd read it in stories – but *this was real*. He really did this – and he wanted to do it to me.

'Are you – we – going to do it now?'

'Not unless you want to. If you do, I'll punish you now for spilling the coffee and you can see what it feels like. If not, I'll draw up a contract first and we'll talk about what you want and don't want and we'll go from there. Which would you like to do?'

I drew my tongue along my bottom lip and saw his jaw tense.

Was it me affecting him so much, or just being in this room? It was certainly having a startling effect on me.

Deep between my legs I felt like I was on fire. It was a crucial moment. A lot of things hung in the balance here.

I chose my words with care. 'I think – I'd like to taste what you do. And if I don't like it I'll leave.'

His eyes widened, like I'd surprised him.

Did I sound assertive? Did his girlfriends never question this setup?

'*Leave?* What, for good?'

I held his gaze. 'For good.'

He looked thoughtful for a moment as if the idea of me leaving had never in a million years occurred to him. That threw me a little.

This was still a one-off, surely? What did he expect?

'Fair enough.' He led me over to the bench and within two minutes I was securely strapped down, wrists and ankles cuffed to the floor, legs wide, ass in the air.

As he worked he became remote, absorbed, and when he spoke it was from somewhere else, like a voice-over on TV. He almost quivered with excitement. From where I was lying, I could see he was very erect.

He caught the direction of my glance and grinned.

'You'll get up close and personal afterwards. First, to business. You'll get six strokes of the belt and you'll accept them in silence. If you cry out you'll get six more. Understood?'

'Don't I have a safeword or something?'

He stood next to me, his erection looming in my face. Then he turned away and I heard the rail on the wall clatter a little as he selected one of the items hanging from it. There was a faint swishing sound, the hiss of leather. He drew it through his fingers and then trailed the end of it along my back towards my splayed ass.

I writhed like a cat. The touch was so sinuous, so gentle.

So unexpected.

'We'll discuss etiquette and permissions and limits when we go through your contract. For now you can use the word "finish" and I will stop. Got that?'

'Yes.'

I felt a snap on my left buttock as the end of the strap made contact. It stung like mad, and it occurred to me that I was still tender from last night's spanking.

Maybe this wasn't such a good idea.

Too late now.

'Yes what?' He was waiting, standing over me with the strap in his hand, and he wanted me to say something.

My mind raced. 'Yes, *sir*.'

'That's better.'

125

He gave me six strokes. I gasped and bucked, desperate not to cry out and earn another six. By the fourth I felt sweat dripping off my jaw from the effort of clenching my teeth, but I did manage it.

When he'd finished he leaned over and put his face close to mine, all concern. 'Now you know. So tell me, are you leaving?'

I was still gasping for breath. I felt like a chicken trussed and ready for the oven and my backside felt like I'd already been roasted, and so did somewhere else. The blows had been harsh, the pain much, much worse than a sting, for sure, but each one had fired something else, something very, very exciting.

I was aroused.

'No, sir.'

For a long minute all I could hear was his jagged breathing, as if he'd just run a race, and then he leaned over and kissed me on the back of the neck. His lips felt hot and wet – and so did I.

'Good. Now I want you to thank me.'

He stood in front of me, legs astride and instantly I knew what I had to do. As I took him in my mouth I wondered if I'd manage him. All the night before I'd marvelled at his size as he'd plunged inside me, over and over.

But now, as I opened my throat to take him deep, I knew that I wanted very much to do this right.

I looked up at him while he pushed in deeper. He

paused with his cock filling my mouth and smiled down at me. 'See how good we are together, Calliope?'

* * *

It's been glorious.

Next day he drew up a contract for me to sign and gave me a list of rules and their penalties. It was great fun going through the list. I was throbbing for him by the time we'd finished. He must have found it pretty exciting too because the minute I'd signed he took me straight up to the office and gave me the first flogging I'd ever had in my life and slammed his cock into me there and then.

I gave up my job to work for him from home. I fit work into my other duties, supervising calls, taking messages, preparing notes for his meetings, organising his cleaning and security staff, preparing his meals and getting ready for when he comes home.

I get disciplined three times a week, and punishments on other nights unless I'm too sore. He's very careful not to overdo things. For two days a week I'm not allowed clothes, so if we're invited out or I've forgotten something in the shops I have to tell him and that earns a punishment.

I'm on my toes all day, trying to juggle all my work with all his requirements. Any slip counts as an offence, so the punishments soon build up. The floggings take the longest, because he has such an expert touch. He can keep me poised on the brink for hours and I get very sensitive.

After a particularly intense session on my breasts, say, or my inner thighs, I can get pretty weepy – even worse than after a caning, which hurts more but lasts only a few minutes.

He soothes me afterwards. He says as my Dom he has a duty of care. Sometimes a session in the medical room, where he gently tends my sore backside, massaging it with creams, or fondles my tormented nipples after repeatedly snatching off the clamps, is so arousing it brings on more tears than the most severe caning. And then the *sex* …

* * *

But this week even the discipline falls flat.

Take last night. He cuffed me to the trapeze for well over an hour with my legs splayed wide and cuffed to the floor. Then he just sat and watched. He had a riding crop over his knees but instead of teasing me with it until I cried out for more he just flexed it now and then and made some phone calls.

When he finally released me he carried me to our room and tethered me to the bed, gagged and blindfolded. He kissed me all over while I mewed helplessly against the gag and then he buried his head between my legs and devoured me.

Within minutes I was building to a massive climax. He knew I was close because he pulled away and untied the blindfold and the gag and then slid inside, ramming into me, his first thrust sending a wave of orgasm crashing over me. The spasms went on and on, and after I'd finished he held me tight until I fell asleep.

Luscious. It was hours ago, I'm still aglow but I feel there was something missing. Where was the spice, the *bite*?

And now I'm getting jumpy. I need the endorphins. I'm going to pieces without proper discipline. I'm dropping things, making real mistakes.

Today I forgot to leave fresh flowers in his en-suite and instead of marching me straight up to the office for a belting – three strokes instantly for sloppy management, an addition to the list for the next punishment night – he just reached for his notepad and wrote down another number.

* * *

While I serve his meal I take a long look at the options. Maybe he's busy at work. Maybe there's some crisis on and he's simply preoccupied. But then, he's always busy at work. It can't be that.

Then an awful possibility dawns – *he's found some-body else.*

The thought terrifies me.

He frowns at me across the table. 'Are you OK, Calliope? You're looking a little pale tonight.'

I smile brightly. 'I'm fine, truly.'

I tremble with anticipation. This is one of the nights I'm not allowed to speak. If I do so, even if he asks me to, I earn a punishment.

Will he notice? Does he even care?

Apparently not. He says nothing, but jots down another number on the pad. During meals he's started keeping it by his plate.

I watch him eat. Will he complain about the half-raw carrots? I served them deliberately to test his reaction.

Zilch.

When I serve his dessert, a fragrant raspberry Pavlova, I hesitate before slipping under the table. This, too, risks a whipping. I have to skip dessert as I'm slimming. While he eats his I must kneel between his knees and pleasure him with my mouth.

But he hardly notices my hesitation, and when I finally kneel he's already finishing the last crumbs of meringue and it's time to clear away.

As I stack the things in the dishwasher the awful truth dawns.

He doesn't love me any more.

It's a terrible blow, but it's the only possible explanation.

With tears running down my face I finish clearing away the things. Everything seems blurred, even my role here. Blindly I stumble up to my room, pull open cupboard doors and stuff some clothing into a bag.

In the mirror I look like a glamour model, all slinky heels, gleaming, curled hair, saucy outfit. Inside I feel like a wet rag.

This isn't working any more. He doesn't want me.

I tear off my outfit and pull on a pair of jeans, an old sweater and a sensible pair of trainers. I have a little money and my credit cards, but no paper for a note. I'd better leave him my mobile number, I suppose – then I realise he knows it already. In fact he's got my mobile, so a swift getaway is not an option.

Best be open about this, go downstairs and tell him straight.

As I leave my room I see his office door is open, so hesitantly I knock, then peep round the door.

He's not there.

In fact the whole apartment is quiet – where is he?

I step into his office, my heart turning over at the sight of the spanking bench and all the equipment. Oh, the happy hours we've spent in here. The anticipation, the fear, the *release* – I swallow and tears well up again.

Angrily I fight them back.

On the desk I see his notepad. Curious, I glance through

it. All I can see are the numbers he's been writing all week. *Why?*

It's a terrible reminder of a ghastly week. But I mustn't cry again, I've got to find him.

Just then he walks in. I freeze, because being in here without permission is a big, big deal and once, back in happier times, could have proved very painful.

He stands very still and looks at me, his expression shocked. 'What are you doing here? And why are you dressed like that?'

'I'm leaving. You don't love me any more.'

He frowns. '*What?*'

Helplessly, I gesture towards the desk and the odious notepad. 'The numbers – you just write things down – you don't punish me properly – you don't even *see* me –'

I break off, overcome. The tears well up again.

With a swift movement he steps up close and locks his arms around me. His eyes burn into mine. 'Tell me, Calliope, what day is it?'

I stare up at him wildly. 'Day? How should I know? Thursday?'

He kisses away my tears and tightens his grip. 'It's the day before our anniversary. Had you forgotten? Tomorrow we'll have been together for a whole year.'

Hope surges but I frown. I still don't understand. 'What about those numbers?' I whisper. 'And what happened to all the discipline?'

He kisses me again and hugs me close, his eyes dancing, alive with excitement. 'You're always cooped up here. You really need a break. We're going to a place in the country with a professional dungeon all to ourselves. I thought it might be fun to have some punishments to be getting on with.'

He points to the contract pinned up over the desk. Below it is a scale of punishments – 'breakages, four strokes of the strap – insolence, six strokes of the cane' – there are twenty.

The list is numbered.

Joy and relief flood through me. 'The numbers on your pad are *punishments*?'

He smiles his full-on, film-star, megawatt smile. 'Yep. Got it in one.'

Oops.

And I thought he'd stopped loving me.

I lean up to kiss him and he claims my mouth, all honey and spice. When he pulls away he presses me close and I bury my face in his chest.

Pierson's Beautiful Cock
Ashley Hind

Pierson has a beautiful cock.

That's what it says, etched deep into the wooden fence-post next to the garage block behind the shopping parade. I should know because I wrote it. I did it five years ago, long before I had any real knowledge of what his dangly bits actually looked like, or those of any other lad for that matter. I just needed to write it, to give substance to the stuff of my fantasies. It wasn't even to show off to my friends. I snuck out one evening and did it alone, nervous almost to the point of distraction that I might get caught in the act. Just seeing my handiwork made me tremble; it was almost like having him in me. Carving that one word 'cock' had the breath faltering in my chest and the blood fizzing through my veins, like his rigid tool was actually there before my eyes. I could barely stand up. It was all I could do to finish before running home to lock myself in my room.

It is still visible today, although the stark yellow of freshly exposed timber that is still ingrained in my mind's eye has weathered. Tellingly no one has added any kind of rebuttal, clearly because Pierson was and constantly remains a Sex God, to me and to a multitude of others. Now that vampires are back in vogue and black-haired, pale-skinned, brooding males are much admired, you can probably add countless more to the list. But I wanted him all along. It was he who was elected to take my virginity on my eighteenth birthday. He who ended up, albeit accidentally, introducing me to my penchant for a very particular kind of bondage fetish, thus bringing rapture to a land of frustration. Three years later, to the very day, he is to come to me again. This time, after all my years of waiting, I am finally going to get my fill of him.

* * *

I can use the word 'bondage' these days with impunity. It holds no fear for me as it once did because I understand it now. In fact, say it enough times and it becomes as benign and essentially ridiculous as all those other '–idge' words, like 'porridge' or 'sausage'. *The name's Bondage. James Bondage.* Once upon a time, before I was in the know, I thought it a dark word, a black word. It conjured thoughts of secret unspeakable kinks, of whips and racks and mediaeval tortures. The image

135

of slavery was there but mostly buried beneath thoughts of pain and ravished flesh. I wonder how many others still assume that to be 'into bondage' must mean you are either a sadist or a masochist? That you take your pleasure by torchlight, within dark dungeons, dressed in leather? Perhaps everyone by now has seen the light.

I have no appetite for pain. I live to be restrained but I have no desire to be thrashed, caned, singed with candle wax, shocked with electric prongs or even tickled. Popular culture may these days allow our heroes to be pain-givers but to me there will always be something sinister about someone who takes pleasure from hurting others. It is not something I think we should normalise. To me, bondage is not about darkness and suppression. It is about a wonderful sunrise within your soul, an awakening, a freeing of your sexual spirit. To me the word no longer appears black in my mind's eye, but gold. Perhaps this is because I 'suffer' from a rather particular affliction.

I am, you see, an insatiable masturbator, a wanka-holic. There is probably a genuine medical name for it, like *megafrigomania*, or something – I haven't actually checked. Some might say the medical name for it is 'being young' but there are specifics to my problem beyond frequency. If I see or think of anything that makes me horny – and my imagination is always searching for things that will – I feel a compulsion to act on it *immediately*, almost as if I have to damp down the rising fire of lust through masturbation. I cannot allow the desire to build; I have to get my hand in my knickers.

The action is frantic. It's a race to finish myself off before the thoughts can bloom and grow. It always leads to a release but a premature one, a forced one, an unsatisfactory one. It is like I am tearing the climax from my body rather than letting it wash over me. It produces a dullness rather than a glow. It leaves bitterness and frustration rather than a contented smile. I cannot just sit on my hands. The urge to act overtakes me. I've tried everything, used all sorts of toys, but they just get cast aside if they don't act quickly enough and my fingers become their customary blur on my poor little puss. The key point is I don't have a compulsion to masturbate as such. I have a compulsion to act on my rude imaginings, almost as if my body is embarrassed that I'm having them, and the only way to do this is through masturbation.

To compound this I have a dirty mind. Many things, even abstract ones, can set me off. Once, when out strolling with a friend on a sunny day, a proper rambling type passed us in the opposite direction. He was OK looking, with nicely tanned muscular legs, but that was by the by. The point was that I had already had an image of him demanding to fuck us both in that field, and so barely two minutes later I was squatting behind a hedge on the pretence that I needed to pee, just to rub the urges away. I could have spent the whole walk in secret glee, embellishing on the scenario, building up the back story before picturing my friend and me side by side on our knees with him swapping between us. Instead, before he was even out of sight, I was hiding in the undergrowth, wrenching out my sneaky orgasm.

I have masturbated in alleyways and telephone boxes, in the back seat of a friend's car and under tables in nightclubs. I have had to drag my hand out of knickers and run to stop me doing it completely out in the open, by some garages, just because etching the words 'Pierson' and 'cock' in the same sentence got me so het up. Once, in a pub, an unidentified female with a chubby bottom crammed into tight jeans bent over about two feet from where I was sitting. I saw the scraps of her diamante-encrusted whale-tail and maybe a third of her voluptuous behind. I remember actually slapping the table with my palms in my rush to push the chair away and get to the toilet. Just from that portion of female bum and its proximity to my face! I had to pretend to my friends I had an upset tummy, to cover my hurried exit.

There may be no prevention, but there is something of a cure, albeit a temporary one. If I cannot get my hand in my knickers, I cannot douse the fire within. The thoughts and images are thus free to blossom. If you forcibly tie me, you set me free. You allow the pleasure to gather and build way beyond anything my body would allow if left to its own devices. You can give me the kind of wonderfully shivering, sweeping releases I automatically rob myself of. That is why to me bondage is now ever golden.

My first experience of it could easily have been a disaster rather than the epiphany it proved to be. There I was on the bed in just knickers and bra, almost delirious with the prospect of surrendering my virginity to the man of my dreams, on the very day I was officially welcomed into adulthood. Pierson had those thick chrome rings on and was dressed in black as always, his shirt unbuttoned almost all the way down. This wasn't specifically for my benefit. He arrived like that. He always seemed to arrive at gatherings thus – certainly the only male in these parts who could do so without getting run out of town or kicked to death for such pretentious affectations. The bell would sound and he would be there, draped against the doorframe, smouldering. The skin of his face and chest would show white against the rest of his blackness, and all the girls would coo and hatch instant secret plans to murder any rivals to his heart.

Of course it wasn't me who got him there. I had no chance of that. It was all down to Madeleine, the only person I have ever thought the equal of Pierson – a true Sex Goddess even back then and one of the very few he gave any respect to. I hadn't even meant to invite her to my birthday gathering, since she had been in the year above me and outside my usual circle. However, she came into the deli where I worked at weekends. She seemed to like me for some reason, and I always found it impossible not to volunteer information of any kind to her, even if she didn't ask for it. So, having told her about the party, I had to invite her.

'I shall bring Pierson,' she said. 'I shall have him break you in.'

Well, despite the equine images this produced, I was still beaming at her and clearly enraptured enough for her to want to make good the promise. I wasn't there at the negotiations. I could picture her going to him, telling him she needed a favour. I could see him trying to bring my face to mind out of the sea of fawning females, deducing that I was reasonably blemish-free and not bad looking with make-up on. Certainly with a bit more to grab hold of than most of the pale waifs endlessly wafting around him. Probably more 'normal' too; less suicidal. He would have checked his diary before agreeing to do me this honour.

So to the night in question: we had barely kissed and he used the time to strip me of my top and skirt. He put me on the bed and climbed on, smiling knowingly down at me. Then he asked if he could tie me. I said yes, or at least gasped it. I was too overwhelmed and flustered to even begin to think what it might mean. He was a Sex God so it had to be OK. He bound me to the headboard with silk ties found in my father's wardrobe (my parents rather rashly having gone out to allow me the freedom of their house now I was an adult). Only when I was bound did he suddenly decide he needed to collect us some more alcohol from the kitchen for the evening, since he planned on spending a good long while with me.

As it happened he didn't return. I found out later that he had been waylaid at the fridge by another girl jealous of his attentions towards me. Maybe she was better looking than I but that's not why he stayed. He stayed because she was flirting outrageously and he saw an opportunity to exert control, and that is the thing that always makes him tick. He informed this boy-stealing beauty that if she wanted him, she would have to suck him off, right there in the kitchen, in front of all those onlookers. She wasn't the type one would assume would comply, but she was tipsy and randy and scared of losing face, so she got on her knees and did his bidding, even collecting a nice round of applause at the end for swallowing it all down.

In his absence I should have been panicky and perhaps outraged, although I didn't then know of his slight. Instead I was like an inferno. The longer I had to think about what he could do to me on his return, the hotter I got. The more I imagined his cock coming out of his trousers and sliding into me, the more I writhed and wriggled and yearned to sate the burn in my clit. The longer I realised I was there at his mercy – at the mercy of *anyone* who should walk in – the more it turned me on. I was raging with the shame, squirming from the vulnerability of my position, but getting ever more excited as the minutes ticked by. His absence was a beautiful torture and in truth at least half of me was hoping he would stay away and let my thoughts and passion build.

In the end it was Madeleine who came to me. I was in such a mess by then I couldn't even speak. I didn't actually need to; she could see the state my bonds had put me in. She didn't free me immediately. Instead she freed my bra and sucked upon each stiff nipple in turn, those touches alone almost enough to drive me over the edge. Then she went down, licking first above my knickers before sliding them aside to get at my bare wetness. Her fingers slipped in me, her hot mouth closed over my clit, and I came. The orgasm was colossal. It was life-changing.

When she came up again she kissed me softly. She nibbled at my neck and ear as she dragged her skirt up and her panties down. I bent my knees up and dug my heels into her bottom to try and make her grind against me. I could already feel another rise of desire coming on. She whispered in my ear, asking if it was the ties that made me come so hard. I said yes, and prayed she would not free me too soon. She showed me that it was only a single knot, which I could have untied at any time. I was so relieved I hadn't known this. She asked if she was the first person to ever make me come. I could barely manage a nod, because she was already squashing her soft cunt to my own.

pricks and of being fucked by them. I just had to lie there and listen and watch and imagine.

She let herself come before she stripped me of my jeans and knickers. She got on top of me. She kissed me just once, to remind me how wonderful it was that first time. She didn't grind or press. She just stayed still, whispering in my ear, talking specifically of Pierson's beautiful prick, of the treat that had so nearly been my birthday present. This would be her favourite topic over [?] months and years, the thing she knew got me most [?] up, and it never failed. I never once felt jealous that [?] knew Pierson's prick so well, I simply felt ecstatic [?] all about it, to let me picture it one more time. [?] to buck up against her but she just lifted her [?] resisted all but a light contact between our bare [?] told me how Pierson loved to be in control, [?] ople up gave him that control. For him it [?] mastery. He adored making girls do rude [?] If a girl refused him anything he would [?] one in a second. Madeleine quietly, [?] of the time she first made out with [?] orgeous erect cock in her hand and

[?]e to suck this for you?'

[?]et that in your mouth,' he had [?]urance, 'until you bend over

'Then you are mine now,' she said, and I was.

* * *

For three years this has remained so. You might think our arrangement strange but I am a slave to her and what she does to me. She has never actually told me I couldn't see other people but I just take it that I shouldn't. I am not her girlfriend, merely one of the many males and females that make up her bevy of playthings. There are no flowers or secret kisses or nights cuddled up together reading the same book. We don't share each other's lives much outside of sex. She's not even a 'Mistress' – not in the sense of one who dominates another's every move and takes pleasure from their abjection. She just lets me know when she is free to be seen and I go, ever willingly. In the meantime I exist completely without her and still quash my rude thoughts in the same unsatisfactory manner.

She understands my need absolutely. She loves to see just how much of a bubbling, burbling mess she can bring me too. She thrives on depriving me because she revels in the state I get in. The longer she keeps me like this, the more she knows my dirty thoughts are building, and the more hers do too. She loves to dream up new methods to get me squirming. In that sense she adores her control over me, the fact that she can just lie there whispering rude things in my ear as

I writhe and beg and practically scream in my need to be made to come.

She hasn't ever felt the urge to whip or cane me. She uses no instruments upon me other than her extensive range of vibrators. She doesn't slap me or spatter me or force me to kiss her feet. I am not compelled or even asked to commit degrading acts for her benefit. God knows she *tells* me of all the humiliations she will heap upon my person, but she doesn't act upon her threats. In my head, sometimes even out loud, I *beg* her to do these things to me, but she just smiles and keeps me bound, and keeps me ever raging.

In essence all I have to do is turn up, let her tie or cuff my wrists and then lie back while she goes to work. She barely even needs to touch me. Just that simple act of restriction makes all the world of difference. She draws pleasures and emotions from me that I cannot quantify. I feel safe and bold and brilliantly alive. It still seems so strange to me that organisms as massively complex and developed as humans can be rendered useless and vulnerable so simply. She need only tie my wrists to ' headboard or secure them behind my back and I a. completely at her mercy.

The first time she tied me was with the soft cotton belt from her dressing gown. She met me at a coffeehouse first and had me tell her all my wanky secrets, which I did without much cajoling. In return she told me what

she liked most: fucking with nasty boys; fucking with pretty girls; teasing; talking dirty; watching girls come; making girls come; me. She was so gorgeous and funny, so comfortable with the subject of sex, it just eliminated all barriers. I felt no trepidation. I just wanted to hav' her recreate that first time she came to me.

I lay down on her bed still clothed and o' my wrists without question. It was, afte benefit. She fastened them individually ' rial around the back of her iron couldn't touch myself. She sai ankles because she loved t my thighs together in asked her what trusted her i

She di just

'Then you are mine now,' she said, and I was.

* * *

For three years this has remained so. You might think our arrangement strange but I am a slave to her and what she does to me. She has never actually told me I couldn't see other people but I just take it that I shouldn't. I am not her girlfriend, merely one of the many males and females that make up her bevy of playthings. There are no flowers or secret kisses or nights cuddled up together reading the same book. We don't share each other's lives much outside of sex. She's not even a 'Mistress' – not in the sense of one who dominates another's every move and takes pleasure from their abjection. She just lets me know when she is free to be seen and I go, ever willingly. In the meantime I exist completely without her and still quash my rude thoughts in the same unsatisfactory manner.

She understands my need absolutely. She loves to see just how much of a bubbling, burbling mess she can bring me too. She thrives on depriving me because she revels in the state I get in. The longer she keeps me like this, the more she knows my dirty thoughts are building, and the more hers do too. She loves to dream up new methods to get me squirming. In that sense she adores her control over me, the fact that she can just lie there whispering rude things in my ear as

I writhe and beg and practically scream in my need to be made to come.

She hasn't ever felt the urge to whip or cane me. She uses no instruments upon me other than her extensive range of vibrators. She doesn't slap me or spatter me or force me to kiss her feet. I am not compelled or even asked to commit degrading acts for her benefit. God knows she *tells* me of all the humiliations she will heap upon my person, but she doesn't act upon her threats. In my head, sometimes even out loud, I *beg* her to do these things to me, but she just smiles and keeps me bound, and keeps me ever raging.

In essence all I have to do is turn up, let her tie or cuff my wrists and then lie back while she goes to work. She barely even needs to touch me. Just that simple act of restriction makes all the world of difference. She draws pleasures and emotions from me that I cannot quantify. I feel safe and bold and brilliantly alive. It still seems so strange to me that organisms as massively complex and developed as humans can be rendered useless and vulnerable so simply. She need only tie my wrists to her headboard or secure them behind my back and I am completely at her mercy.

The first time she tied me was with the soft cotton belt from her dressing gown. She met me at a coffeehouse first and had me tell her all my wanky secrets, which I did without much cajoling. In return she told me what she liked most: fucking with nasty boys; fucking with pretty girls; teasing; talking dirty; watching girls come; making girls come; me. She was so gorgeous and funny, so comfortable with the subject of sex, it just eliminated all barriers. I felt no trepidation. I just wanted to have her recreate that first time she came to me.

I lay down on her bed still clothed and offered up my wrists without question. It was, after all, for my benefit. She fastened them individually, looping the material around the back of her iron headboard so that I couldn't touch myself. She said she would never tie my ankles because she loved to watch me wriggle and squeeze my thighs together in my horny frustration. I never once asked her what she planned to do to me once tied. I trusted her implicitly.

She didn't even touch me for the first half hour. She just stayed beside me, poring over photos of erections in a dirty magazine, showing them to me, talking excitedly about how they would feel in her hand, in her mouth, deep up her pussy or her bottom. Her eyes shone when she spoke of them. She was so in love with cocks I couldn't believe she could sacrifice even a minute of her time with me when she could have had any cock in town at the click of her fingers. Her hunger for them was so palpable I could almost taste one – something I had yet to do in reality. She stripped until she was fabulously naked beside me and masturbated while she talked of pricks and of being fucked by them. I just had to lie there and listen and watch and imagine.

She let herself come before she stripped me of my jeans and knickers. She got on top of me. She kissed me just once, to remind me how wonderful it was that first time. She didn't grind or press. She just stayed still, whispering in my ear, talking specifically of Pierson's beautiful prick, of the treat that had so nearly been my birthday present. This would be her favourite topic over the months and years, the thing she knew got me most het up, and it never failed. I never once felt jealous that she knew Pierson's prick so well, I simply felt ecstatic to hear all about it, to let me picture it one more time.

I tried to buck up against her but she just lifted her hips and resisted all but a light contact between our bare quims. She told me how Pierson loved to be in control, how tying people up gave him that control. For him it was all about mastery. He adored making girls do rude things for him. If a girl refused him anything he would be onto the next one in a second. Madeleine quietly, unhurriedly told me of the time she first made out with him. She had that gorgeous erect cock in her hand and she said to him,

'I expect you want me to suck this for you?'

'You are not going to get that in your mouth,' he had answered with calm self-assurance, 'until you bend over and show me your anus.'